Corregidora

GAYL JONES

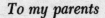

To my parents

Corregidora

I

It was 1947 when Mutt and I was married. I was singing in Happy's Café around on Delaware Street. He didn't like for me to sing after we were married because he said that's why he married me so he could support me. I said I didn't just sing to be supported. I said I sang because it was something I had to do, but he never would understand that. We were married in December 1947 and it was in April 1948 that Mutt came to Happy's drunk and said if I didn't get off the stage he was going to take me off. I didn't move, and some men put Mutt out. While I was singing the first few songs I could see Mutt peeking in, looking drunk and evil, then I didn't see him and thought he'd gone on home and gone to bed to sleep it off. I always left by the back way. You go down some narrow steps and through a short alley and then you be to the Drake Hotel, where Mutt and I was staying then. I said good night and went out back.

"I'm your husband. You listen to me, not to them."

I didn't see him at first because he was standing back in the shadows behind the door. I didn't see him till he'd grabbed me around my waist and I was struggling to get loose.

"I don't like those mens messing with you," he said.

"Don't nobody mess with me."

"Mess with they eyes."

That was when I fell.

The doctors in the hospital said my womb would have to come out. Mutt and me didn't stay together after that. I wouldn't even let him come in the hospital to see me when I knew what was happening. They said he'd come in when I didn't know what was happening. They said when I was delirious I was cursing him *and* the doctors and nurses out.

Tadpole McCormick was the man who owned Happy's Café. Square-jawed and high-cheekboned, he was one of them Hazard, Kentucky, niggers. I was singing in Happy's when Demosthenes Washington owned it, about two years ‑ before Tadpole took it over. I never did know how it got the name Happy's because I never did know anybody named Happy that owned it. Tadpole said he got his name because when he was a kid he was always messing around tadpole holes. He came to see me when I could have visitors.

"How you feeling, U.C.?" He didn't sit down in the chair by the bed but stayed standing.

"Awright."

"They tell me you been doing some hard cussing while you was sick."

"Yeah."

He didn't say anything. I could tell he felt awkward. I asked if he wanted to sit down. He said, "Naw thanks." Then he said, "Well, I just wont to tell you he's been barred from the place, so when you get back he won't be troubling you."

"He's been barred from my place too. What are you doing in the meantime?"

"Got a little combo. Eddy Pace's group."

"Aw."

He said nothing.

"Do you know what's happened?" I asked.

He nodded.

"Do you ever feel as if something was crawling under your skin?"

He nodded again.

"Taddy, will you take me home when it's time to go?"

He said yes.

When it was time to go home he didn't take me back to the Drake. He had three rooms over the café. I slept on a couch that let out as a bed. He slept on the couch that didn't let out. I was still weak and there were the stitches that wouldn't be out for a while. The first meal he fixed me was vegetable soup. He didn't have any. He sat by the bed.

"I'm glad you didn't think 'home' meant the Drake."

"He wasn't barred from the Drake," he said.

The soup was good but I only ate the broth. I kept feeling as if I would throw up.

"I thought you'd want more," he said.

"Naw, I'm not very hungry. My stomach still feels tender, all those liquids they had me on."

It was evening but I didn't hear even any faint music from below.

"Where's the combo?"

"I told them not to come in tonight."

"What about business?"

"You more important than business."

I said nothing. I could tell he felt awkward again. He took the bowl and went back to the kitchen. When he came back he said, "They still come to drink." Then he said, "I'm going downstairs. I'll be back up later to see if you want anything."

"Okay."

He left.

When he came back, I opened my eyes.

"I thought you were sleeping," he said.

"No."

"You should be. How do you feel?"

"Still weak. It's not so much how I feel in my body."

"What do you feel?"

"As if part of my life's already marked out for me—the barren part."

"You can't expect a woman to take something like that easy."

"What about the man?"

"You mean Mutt? You don't intend to go back to him, do you?"

"No, I mean any other man."

"If I were the man it wouldn't matter. I don't know about any other man."

I said nothing. I might have wanted him to say that, but I hadn't intended for him to.

"I feel like sleeping now," I said.

He turned my light out, and went into the next room where the couch was. He closed the door.

I lay on my back, feeling as if something more than the womb had been taken out. When he was downstairs, I'd looked at the stitches across my belly again. When they were gone, I'd get back to work again, that and . . . I couldn't help feeling I was forcing something with Tadpole. What our talk was leading to. Something I needed, but couldn't give back. There'd be plenty I couldn't give back now. Of course, I'd get the divorce from Mutt . . . I went to sleep.

The next morning Tadpole found me staring at the ceiling.

"Didn't you sleep?"

"Yes, I just woke up early that's all."

"They said you could have juice for breakfast. Nothing solid yet."

"You going by their menu?"

"Yeah."

He went into the kitchen and came back with some juice. While I drank, he emptied the bedpan. When he came back, he stood watching me. I was frowning, but I didn't tell him to stop. When I finished, I handed him the glass. He took it back and came back and watched me again.

"What is it, Taddy?"

"Nothing. I'm going down now."

"Okay. Is that what you wanted?"

"I'll be back to check you a little later."

"Okay, Taddy."

He watched me a moment more.

"What is it?"

"The doctor wants you to come back in a couple of weeks for a checkup. I'll take you."

"Okay."

He went downstairs.

When he came back, I'd been sleeping, but woke up as soon as he opened the door.

"Have a good sleep?"

"Yeah."

"Cat Lawson made you some chicken soup."

"Thank her."

"I did."

Catherine Lawson lived across the street from Happy's. She straightened people's hair. She wasn't a regular hairdresser, but people would go to her anyway, and give her a couple of dollars for doing it.

He pulled up the little table and brought me a spoon from the kitchen and took the foil from around the bowl.

"I better get your pill first."

He got the pills and I took one and a little water. I didn't eat the pieces of chicken. My stomach still felt queasy.

"They said you had gastritis too. You weren't eating right."

"I was eating all right."

"Or worrying too much."

"I can't talk to you about it."

"I know most about it already."

"Then I don't have to talk to you about it."

When I finished he moved the table away and took the bowl back in the kitchen.

"She said if you want anything to just send over for it."

"That's sweet of her."

"No, it's not sweet. She cares about you."

"That's good to know."

He touched my forehead.

"They said you had those nurses scared to death of you. Cussing them out like that. Saying words they ain't never heard before. They kept saying, 'What is she, a gypsy?' "

"What did you say?"

"Naw. I said if she's a gypsy I'm a Russian."

"How do you know you ain't? One a them might a got your great-grandmama down in a Volga boat or something."

"Those pills make you silly?"

"I'm already silly."

He said nothing. I said nothing else. He sat down on the edge of the bed.

"Ursa Corre. I know what the 'U' stands for but I keep getting the last one wrong. Corrente. Corredo."

"Corregidora. Old man Corregidora, the Portuguese slave

breeder and whoremonger. (Is that what they call them?) He fucked his own whores and fathered his own breed. They did the fucking and had to bring him the money they made. My grandmama was his daughter, but he was fucking her too. She said when they did away with slavery down there they burned all the slavery papers so it would be like they never had it."

"Who told you all 'at?"

"My great-grandmama told my grandmama the part she lived through that my grandmama didn't live through and my grandmama told my mama what they both lived through and my mama told me what they all lived through and we were suppose to pass it down like that from generation to generation so we'd never forget. Even though they'd burned everything to play like it didn't never happen. Yeah, and where's the next generation?"

He nodded but said nothing.

I asked, "How's Cat?"

"She said she didn't have no complaints. I was passing down the street and she said, 'You got U.C. up there, ain't you?' I said, 'Yeah.' I thought she was going to say something, you know. She said, 'Come on in here. I fixed her up some chicken soup I wont you to take over there. I didn't wont to take it up myself, cause she just got back and women get evil after something like that and I don't like to mess with no evil women. Tell her I be up to see her when she feeling all right.' "

"Yeah, I wondered why she didn't come herself. Tell her I stopped cussing."

"Yeah?"

"Uh hum."

"I went in there and it smell like she had somebody's head on fire . . . They ain't told me shit."

"What?"

"I mean like your grandmama told you. I guess some people just keep things in."

"Well, some things can't be kept in. What I didn't tell you is old man Corregidora fathered my grandmama and my mama too."

Taddy frowned, but he said nothing.

"What my mama always told me is Ursa, you got to make generations. Something I've always grown up with."

Tad said nothing. Then he said, "I guess you hate him then, don't you?"

"I don't even know the bastard."

He frowned and I knew he hadn't meant the old man, but I went on as if he had.

"I've got a photograph of him. One Great Gram smuggled out, I guess, so we'd know who to hate. Tall, white hair, white beard, white mustache, a old man with a cane and one of his feet turned outward, not inward, but outward. Neck bent forward like he was raging at something that wasn't there. Mad Portuguese. I take it out every now and then so I won't forget what he looked like."

"You didn't know who I meant?"

"I didn't know until after you'd said it."

He said nothing. He didn't make me answer. He left me and went downstairs again.

A Portuguese seaman turned plantation owner, he took her out of the field when she was still a child and put her to work in his whorehouse while she was a child. She was to go out or he would bring the men in and the money they gave her she was to turn over to him. There were other women he used like that. She was the pretty little one with the almond eyes and coffee-bean skin, his favorite. "A good little piece. My best. Dorita. Little gold piece."

Great Gram sat in the rocker. I was on her lap. She told the same story over and over again. She had her hands around my waist, and I had my back to her. While she talked, I'd stare down at her hands. She would fold them and then unfold them. She didn't need her hands around me to keep me in her lap, and sometimes I'd see the sweat in her palms. She was the darkest woman in the house, the coffee-bean woman. Her hands had lines all over them. It was as if the words were helping her, as if the words repeated again and again could be a substitute for memory, were somehow more than the memory. As if it were only the words that kept her anger. Once when she was talking, she started rubbing my thighs with her hands, and I could feel the sweat on my legs. Then she caught herself, and stopped, and held my waist again.

". . . He was a big strapping man then. His hair black and straight and greasy. He was big. He looked like one a them coal Creek Indians but if you said he looked like an Indian he'd get mad and beat you. Yeah, I remember the day he took me out of the field. They had coffee there. Some places they had cane and then others cotton and tobacco like up here. Other places they had your mens working down in mines. He would take me hisself first and said he was breaking me in. Then he started bringing other men and they would give me money and I had to give it over to him. Yeah, he had a stroke or something and that's what turned his foot outside. They say he was praying and calling in all his niggers and telling them he'd give them such and such a amount of money if they take it off him but they all said they didn't put it on him. He got well, though, and didn't die. It just turned his foot outside and he behave like he always did. It did something to his neck too, because he always go around like he was looking for something that wasn't there. I don't know how he finally went,

because by then I was up to Louisiana, but I bet he didn't go easy. Yeah, he have that took afterward. I stole it because I said whenever afterward when evil come I wanted something to point to and say, 'That's what evil look like.' You know what I mean? Yeah, he did more fucking than the other mens did. Naw, I don't know what he did with the others."

Sweat inside her hands. Her palms like sunburnt gold.

"Were you sleeping?"

"Naw, I was dreaming."

"About what?"

"I've already told it."

He said nothing. He had boxes with him.

"I brought your things."

"I was going to ask you to, but I didn't want to bother you again."

"I should have thought about it. I didn't think about it till you started talking about that picture."

"Aw. Was *he* there?"

"Naw. He moved out. They said he boxed up your stuff and they put it in storage. They didn't know whether anybody was going to come and get it or not."

"They didn't say where he went?"

"Do you care?"

"Naw. I don't care. Let me see if you've got everything."

"There were only these two."

"I didn't have much."

He put the boxes down in front of me and moved things around as I directed him. Everything was there.

"The photograph's in that brown envelope."

He took it out and looked at it, put it back. He said nothing. He put the boxes at the foot of the bed.

"Tell me when there's anything you need out of them," he said.

"I thought you'd say something," I said.

"He looks like you described him."

"They say they all get crazy when they get old."

"How were you *really* taught to feel about him?" he asked, looking at me hard.

"How I told you," I said, angry.

"My grandmother was white," he said. "She was a orphan and they had her working out in the fields along with the blacks and treated her like she was one. She was a little girl about nine, ten, 'leven. My granddaddy took her in and raised her and then when she got old enough he married her. She called him Papa. And when they were married, she still called him Papa."

"Maybe I should ask you how you were taught to feel."

He said nothing. Then he said, "She never got crazy though. One of the children came out black and the other one came out white. But she never did get crazy though."

I said nothing. I told him when it was time for me to soak in the tub to help the stitches come out he'd have to help me. I told him they thought I was going home with a husband or a sister. He said he'd do whatever I needed done, then he frowned and said he had to go back downstairs again. I asked him what his mama was, but he was already out the door.

"... *His wife was a skinny stuck-up little woman he got from over in Lisbon and had her brought over here. He wouldn't sleep with her, so she made me sleep with her, so for five years I was sleeping with her and him. That was when I was from about thirteen to eighteen. Then she started looking real bad and then she died on account of the climate. But they had me sleeping with both of them.*"

"*You telling the truth, Great Gram?*"

She slapped me.

"*When I'm telling you something don't you ever ask if I'm lying. Because they didn't want to leave no evidence of what they done—so it couldn't be held against them. And I'm leaving evidence. And you got to leave evidence too. And your children got to leave evidence. And when it come time to hold up the evidence, we got to have evidence to hold up. That's why they burned all the papers, so there wouldn't be no evidence to hold up against them.*"

I was five years old then.

There was a knock on the door.

"Come in."

She poked her head in first. A dark, dark woman with straightened hair drawn back and tied with a rubber band. A smooth-complexioned woman, she was close to sixty, but looked forty-five. She came from a family that stayed young-looking.

"Catty, I didn't think you was coming to see me."

"Did Tadpole tell you what I told him?"

"Yeah." I smiled.

"I thought he tell you. I don't like to come around when women have their evil spells."

She was inside now, sitting on the edge of the bed.

"Why? Cause you get evil too?"

She laughed.

"I brought you some more broth," she said, getting up. "I put it in here in the refrigerator, and tell Tadpole to heat it up for you and don't feed it to you when it's cold." She came back from the kitchen and sat back down. "You seen your bastard?"

"Naw. Tadpole said he moved out of the hotel and they don't know where he's gone."

"Well, I see him hanging out in front a the place every evening. He hang around there awhile, peeping in 'cause he can't come in. You know Tadpole barred him from the place?"

I nodded.

"Yeah, well, he peep in and then he go on down the street. He don't say nothing to Tadpole and Tadpole don't say nothing to him. Once I saw him I just come on over across the street and said, 'Mutt, you **ain't** got no business hanging around out here, she don't want to see you.' He looked at me evil—Christ, that man's got evil. He looked at me and didn't say nothing but 'Shit, Miss Lawson.' Now, when have he called me Miss Lawson? He call me Cat like everybody else do. He walked on. So I ain't bother the nigger no more. Just let him stand out there, and walk on when he get ready to walk on."

I was frowning.

"He ain't going to bother you no more. I didn't mean to scare you. I don't think he mean to bother you no more. Just stand out there and get a look. You know how mens are when they do something like that. After they get a look, they just go on away and leave you alone."

"Some of em."

"I didn't mean to scare you."

"I ain't scared."

She looked at me harder than she'd ever looked, then she softened.

"It wasn't just the fall, was it, baby?"

"What do you mean?"

"You was big, wasn't you?"

"He didn't know."

"Did you know?"

"They said I was about a month pregnant, little over a month."

"They tell him?"

"Naw, I don't think so."

"You know which him I'm talking about, don't you?"

I looked away from her.

She said nothing, then got up. "Well, you start to working again things be all right. You got two men evil over you. I passed Tadpole downstairs he act like he didn't want to speak. I ask was you up here. I knew you was. He said Yeah. I asked if you was sleeping. He said Naw, he didn't think you was. But trying to get him to say something was like pulling his teeth, so I just came on upstairs."

She patted my leg through the sheet.

"I got to get back down now, baby. You be all right. I promised Elvira I'd do her hair."

"Awright, thanks for the broth. They gave Tadpole a menu, but I don't think he knows what to do."

"I be checking up on you then. I just wanted to make sure you wasn't evil."

"Naw."

She patted my leg again, and left.

She hadn't been long gone when Tadpole came up.

"What did she want?" he asked.

"She just came to bring me some broth and see how I was feeling. She told me to make sure you heat it up before you fed it to me." I laughed but he didn't.

"Why she stay so long?"

"You know how it is when you get to talking."

"I seen her out there talking to Mutt Thomas the other night."

I frowned. "She was trying to tell him to go away."

"But he wouldn't listen, would he?"

"Naw. Why didn't you tell me he was hanging around out there?"

"I thought you'd find out soon enough. I just didn't want to bother you now."

"Well, I found out."

He started to leave.

"She wasn't saying nothing about you, Tadpole."

"I didn't say she was."

He went out. I turned over and tried to get some sleep.

I stayed there, and when it was time for the stitches to come out, he'd help me into the tub to soak, and then when a half-hour was up, he'd come with a towel and help me out. He'd never stay in the bathroom. Once, after I'd soaked for a half-hour, he knocked and came in with the towel. He helped me out by the arm. He had a way of look- ing without looking, only enough to help me in and out. It was a big thick green towel that covered me down to my knees. I held it around me under my breasts.

"The stitches are about gone," I said. He was still holding my arm. "You haven't seen the scar."

He said he hadn't looked.

"You can feel it," I said. "I can just reach down and feel it. It's going to leave a bad one."

"I reckon," he said, helping me back to the bed. I sat down on the edge of it, drying myself off. He went back to let the water out. He came back and put my feet up. I handed him the towel, and got under the cover.

"You ought to be able to get in and out by yourself."

"It's only so I won't slip," I said.

"The doctor wants to see you again in a couple of days."

"I hope that means real food when I get back."

"Maybe."

He was sitting near the bed and I took his hand and put it under the sheet.

"You can feel it, can't you?"

He said yes. I thought he was going to take his hand away, but he waited for me to.

"It's worse when you touch it than when you look at it."

"I suppose. Most scars are."

I said nothing, then asked, "Has he still been out there?"

"Yeah, he's still out there."

"You haven't said anything?"

"Naw, he's outside. I can't bar him from looking."

"Tell him that 'can't come in' means 'can't look in' either."

He laughed. "I can't tell him that."

"You could make him go away."

"*I* can't make him go away."

"What does that mean?"

"Nothing. He's waiting for you, that's all. See you come out and sing, and know you're all right."

"That's what Cat said. Is that what he said?"

"I ain't talked to him."

"I thought maybe you might have."

"Naw. He looks and I look. He knows I don't want him in here and he don't come."

"My butt."

"What?"

"He ain't come in cause he ain't seen what he wants to see yet."

"He ain't coming in then."

I nodded. "Okay."

He said nothing. He stood up.

"After I see the doctor, I want to see a lawyer," I said.

He nodded. He patted my belly through the cover, and went back to finish cleaning out the tub.

When he came back through, I had my eyes closed. I could feel him bending down, but he must have stopped midway because he didn't finish.

"I'm awake," I said. I didn't open my eyes.

He bent down and kissed me. Then I heard the door close.

"I am going to take you off the pills and see how you feel," the doctor said. He had finished examining me, and I was sitting in the chair near his desk. "If you start getting nauseated again, take them. I want to see you in two more weeks. Is Mr. Corregidora with you?"

"That's *my* name, not my husband's."

"Oh, I see. Is Mr. Thomas with you? When I looked out there I saw a man standing with you. I'd like to see him."

"Naw."

"Aw, okay."

"You can take Mutt's name off there anyway."

"What do you mean?"

"I'm filing suit for divorce."

"Well, when I looked out and saw that man standing there I thought you'd stopped blaming him."

I said nothing, and stood up. When I got outside, Tadpole came over and took my elbow.

"See you in two weeks," the nurse said.

"Okay."

"How'd it go?" Tad asked.

"Awright."

"What do you mean awright?"

"He took me off the pills, unless I get nauseated again."

"What's wrong?"

"Nothing."

We walked to the door.

"He thought you were Mutt," I said quietly. "I mean, my husband. He thought you were Mr. Corregidora."

"What?" He was frowning.

"He didn't know I kept my name and Mutt kept his."

"When do you come back?"

"Two weeks."

"I mean what time?"

"Same time."

"Did he say you could work?"

"I didn't ask. I forgot to. Should I go back and ask?"

"Naw."

"Yes, I'd better," I said. "I was planning to start whether he said so or not."

He took my arm slightly, but I went anyway. We were standing in the door. Tadpole stood aside to let somebody pass. I asked him to wait for me. "Where would I go?" he asked.

When I got back, Tadpole was still frowning.

"What did he say?"

"Anytime I feel like it."

"I'll go ask him myself."

"No. He said anytime I feel like it, after the next two weeks. He said it meant building up time. One hour one night. Maybe hour and a half the next. Like that. Till I build myself back up again."

"I would've asked him if you hadn't told me," he said. "I'll get you a stool."

"I don't work sitting down," I said.

He said nothing, and we got in the car. When I looked over at him, he was looking as if he was mad at me. When he saw me watching him, he looked ahead quickly, and turned on the ignition.

When we got back I said I was tired and wanted to lie down. It was around noon. I'd had a ten o'clock appointment.

"Same time, same position," I said.

"What?"

He was hanging up my sweater and his jacket.

"He had me up on the table so he could look at the scar. Every time you go to the doctor they say, 'Get up on the table' or 'Take your clothes off and get up on the table.' Somebody ought to say Naw."

"That's what Cat did once. She said the man told her, 'Get up on the table.' So she said, 'I told that bastard, Naw, I wasn't getting up on the table. And he didn't make me neither.' "

"How you know?"

"You know Cat talk the same way in front of men as she do women," he said.

"Yeah."

"You know when she was married to Joe Hunn he broke the window out of his car and come in and said, 'Honey, you got a piece of cardboard?' and she went in and got him a Kotex box. He just as silly as she is though. He used it. People said, 'Man, where you get that thing?' Making men laugh and embarrassing women. I don't see why they didn't stay together, cause they was just alike."

"You never can tell," I said.

He said nothing. Then he said, "You know what I mean. Both. Not silly. But bold. You know."

"Bold silly."

"Well . . . How did he say the scar looked?"

"He said it looked good. I said if this supposed to look good I hate to see one supposed to look bad."

He raised up my blouse. "It looks good," he said.

I put my blouse back in my skirt.

"Did you get a chance to talk to the lawyer for me?"

"Yeah. He said he'll take care of it."

"Well, when he gets ready for me to sign anything, tell him I'll be in there to sign it."

"I told him."

I patted his knee. He smiled a little, but said nothing.

"What do you want, Ursa?"

I looked at him with a slight smile that left quickly. "What do you mean?"

"What I said. What do you want?"

I smiled again. "What all us Corregidora women want. Have been taught to want. To make generations." I stopped smiling.

He looked at me. "What do you want, Ursa?"

"More than yourself?"

He raised me and kissed me very hard.

"I'll let you sleep."

"I don't want to sleep."

"Then rest."

"Okay."

"I'll be back up later and fix us something to eat."

"No, I'll do it."

"No, I want to."

"Okay."

He started to go.

"When the doctor gave you that menu for me, who did you say you were?"

"I didn't say."

"Who did he *think* you were?"

He didn't say. He went downstairs.

". . . *The important thing is making generations. They can burn the papers but they can't burn conscious, Ursa. And that what makes the evidence. And that's what makes the verdict.*"

"Procreation. That could also be a slave-breeder's way of thinking."

"But it's not."

"No. And you can't."

"Not anymore, no."

Gram was standing in the doorway looking down at me. She looked tall then, because I was little, but Mama said she wasn't no more than five feet.

". . . His hair was so dark and greasy straight you could a swore he was pure Indian, but if you even dare say something, he stick a poker up your ass, a hot coal poker. Naw, but he wasn't though. He was from over there somewhere in Portugal. Naw, it wasn't Lisbon. That's the capital. Naw, I don't know where. He probably didn't even know where. He was a seaman. Naw, a sea captain. That's why the king give him lands, and slaves and things, but he didn't hardly use nothing but the womens. Naw, he wasn't the first that did it. There was plenty that did it. Make the women fuck and then take their money. And you know sometimes the mistresses was doing it too so they could have little pocket money that their husbands didn't know about. And getting their brothers and their brother's friends and other mens they know, you know, and then they make theyselves right smart money for their purse. Naw, his wife didn't do that. She sleep with you herself. I guess she didn't wont no money. Or didn't need none. Or just figure it was all the same. That hot climate. Nose like a baby hawk. Naw, she couldn't do a damn thing. Naw, she didn't give him nothing but a little sick rabbit that didn't live but to be a day old. So then he just stopped doing it. Naw, she couldn't do a damn thing."

"No, because it depends on if it's for you or somebody else. Your life or theirs."

I wouldn't take my eyes off her. She kept looking down at me.

"What you doing?"
Cat had come in but I hadn't heard her.
"Tadpole said you might be sleeping, but I said I'd just

peep in and see and if you was, I wouldn't bother you. He's got right evil these days."

"Yeah. Naw, I wasn't sleeping."

"Just thinking?"

"Yeah."

"I seen you staring wide-eyed at the ceiling, and didn't know if I should disturb that either."

"Naw, come on in."

She came in.

"It's nothing," I said.

She came and sat down on the bed.

"You okay? How did it go with the doctor?"

"He took me off the pills. He wonts me to come back in a couple of weeks though, and then I think I can start working again after that."

"It be good to hear you sing again. Eddy Pace was trash and all they doing down there now is wining and dining. I should say whiskeying."

"I'm sorry. I wish I wasn't being so much trouble to him."

"I didn't mean nothing by you."

"If he didn't have me up here he'd be having a band in."

"Aw, that nigger don't care. He rather have you up here anyway."

I said nothing, then I said, "But seriously, if I don't start feeling better in another week can I come stay with you?"

"Sure. You could've come stayed with me anytime. I just figured things was settled here."

"No."

She said nothing, then patted my knee. "Well, you be awright."

"Mutt still out there?"

"Yeah."

"Yeah, Tad said he was."

"Why you ask me then?"

"No reason."

She looked at me hard.

"Tad's seeing a lawyer for me about the divorce and when he gets ready I have to sign the papers."

"You got Tad seeing him for you?"

"Yeah, why?"

"No reason."

I looked at her, then I said, "I think maybe we might get together, you know, after all this is over."

"Then you don't want to move in with me."

"Yeah, you know, till I'm feeling better. I don't want to be a burden to him."

"You want to be one to me," she said.

I didn't answer.

"Okay," I said finally.

"Okay, what?"

"Okay, I'll stay here."

"Naw, I think it be better if you was over to my place. Sooner the better. But seem like to me you already together. People think you already together."

"Naw, we not. He's been a good friend. I don't care what people think anyway. I never have."

"What Mutt think?"

"Naw, nor what Mutt think. I told you that story. From the day he throwed me down those stairs we not together, and we not coming back together."

"It was an accident."

"You sound like if he was sitting here what he be saying. 'Aw, honey, I was drunk. Aw, honey, it was a accident. I didn't mean to do it. You know I wouldn't've done it. You know I'm sorry. All I wanted to do was take care of you like a husband should.' Now, what good am I for a man?"

"Why don't you ask Tadpole that?"

I told her to go to hell.

She said she was, if I promised I was still coming back with her.

I said nothing.

"Listen, honey, I'ma tell you something seem like you don't know or play like you don't know. Right now's not the time for you to be grabbing at anything. Any woman to be grabbing at anything. Out of fear. I don't know what. Ask yourself how did you feel about Tadpole before all of this happened. I know he's being good to you, but this is a rush job. Just thinking about the two of y'all getting together is a rush job. You know what I mean? He's looked at you and seem like you scared somebody else won't. You a beautiful woman. They be many mens that . . ."

I told her to shut up.

She looked hurt, then she looked evil. "Just listen, will you?" She didn't give me time to say if I would or I wouldn't. "You be taking what you need, but do you think you be giving him what he need?"

I said nothing. She got up and went to the door. Then she said, "But even he can't give you everything you need." Without turning around, she went out the door.

When Tadpole came upstairs to fix us lunch, I said, "I'm going over to Cat's."

He didn't make any of the expressions I thought he would make.

"Do you want me to take you?" he asked.

"Naw, I can take myself," I said.

"I'll take you," he said. "You'll have something to eat first."

"I can get something to eat over there."

"Well, you not." He left me and went back in the kitchen.

"Did Cat Lawson say anything to you?" I asked.

"She said you be staying over there now till you get back up on your feet."

"That all?"

"Yeah."

He brought me some lunch.

"Ain't you eating?"

"Naw, I had something downstairs."

When I finished eating, and was ready to leave, he had one of the boxes and me by the arm and said he'd bring the other box over later.

"Do I get visiting privileges?" he asked as we were going out the door.

"As many as you want."

When we got there, Cat was straightening Jeffy's hair. Jeffy was the girl who stayed with her when her mother worked and sometimes when her mother wasn't working. She couldn't have been more than fourteen. Cat was telling her to hold back her ear when we came in and was straightening along the edge.

"I didn't expect y'all so soon," she said.

"I thought you did," I said.

"Which room she got?" Tadpole asked.

"That one in there," said Cat, nodding to the room to the right of the living room.

"You burned me," Jeffy said.

"Hush."

The house had three other rooms, a kitchen and another bedroom and a bathroom, off to the other side of the living room. That room was the only one on that side. I saw a slop jar over in the corner.

Tadpole took the box back in the bedroom. I followed him in.

"Tadpole, turn back the bed for her, will you? My hands greasy."

"I can do it," I said.

"Tadpole do it."

"Ow," Jeffy said.

"I said hush."

"You burned me."

"Hold your ear. If you'd hold your ear like I told you to I wouldn't a burned you."

"I'm going back and get the other box," Tadpole said.

"Okay."

"Now you can let go," Cat said to Jeffy.

I came back in the front room. Cat was doing the back.

"Ain't you better get undressed and get in bed," she told me.

"I thought I'd sit up for a while," I said, sitting down on the couch.

"What the doctor say?"

"He said whatever I feel like doing."

"I know he didn't say that."

"As long as I don't overdo it."

"Well, you overdone it. Go get in the bed."

"You not my . . ."

"What?"

"Nothing."

"I seen your Sweet Daddy," Jeffy said.

"Hush," Cat said.

"What?"

"I'm just telling her I seen her Sweet Daddy."

"I said to hush up."

"He look like he haven't shaved in about a week."

Cat hit her up side the head, and she jumped out of the chair, crying, and ran out.

"You better get your ass on back in here, girl," Cat said.

"Tha's awright," I said.

"She be back," Cat said.

"I'ma tell Mama," Jeffy sobbed.

"I'ma tell your mama," Cat said. "Now get your ass on back in here."

Jeffy came back in and sat down. There were tears in her eyes, but she wasn't making any noise.

"You don't get twenty-five and automatically be a woman neither," Cat said to me. "You better get *yours* in there too."

I got up and went in the bedroom. I didn't feel like getting evil.

"That how old she is?" Jeffy asked.

"Yeah."

"She don't look it."

Tadpole came back with the other box. He started out without saying anything.

"Make the first visiting day soon," I said softly.

He nodded, and went out.

Cat came to close the bedroom door.

"If these niggers start worrying you," she said, "I might have to move you in the back bedroom."

I said nothing. She closed the door.

About fifteen minutes later, she opened the door again.

"That baby's hard, ain't she? She gone down to her mama's now. She be back up here though, cause Lurene got to work tonight. They put her on the night shift down to the factory."

"Aw."

"They just shifting her every whicha way. I said if I was her I wouldn't stand for it."

"If she didn't stand for it she wouldn't have a job."

"Well, I'm glad I do what I do. I ain't got a license, but leastwise I keep my own hours. And your job, you know. Something like that."

"I don't keep my own hours," I said.

"But you doing something you like doing. You got a

talent. A talent or a craft, that's what I say, and don't have those sons of a bitches hanging on your neck all the time. And daughters of bitches. When I was young I worked in white women's kitchens, so I know how it is. Leastwise the factory ain't a kitchen, but ain't much different. Still got the devil on your back. Leastwise you like what you do."

"Yeah, I like it . . . There's always something you can do to keep your own hours."

"Now we ain't talking about that."

I laughed. "Well . . ."

"Hush."

She sat down in the chair next to the front-room door.

"I suppose I don't *mind* what I do. It ain't like when I was young though, you know."

"You don't seem old."

"I don't know too many people that *seem* old . . . Well, I better get up from here and leave you alone. Talking about niggers bothering you." She got up again. "Something I can get you?"

"Naw, thanks."

"Well, I let you rest. If you wont something, just holler."

I said I would.

"He leave you alone, didn't he?"

"Who?"

"Tadpole."

"Yeah, he left me alone." I frowned at her. She frowned back, and closed the door again. Then she peeped back in the door.

"What the doctor say you can eat?"

"Anything."

"I fry you some chicken then for supper."

"Good."

She closed the door.

I settled back in the double bed, and pulled the covers

up to my neck. The bed was high and it was a large empty room, except for a cedar chest and a wardrobe. There was a window facing the street, with dingy white-lace curtains. I slept.

I woke up to the smell of scorched hair and fried chicken. There was a tap on the door. I said, "Come in." It was Jeffy.

"Miss Catherine wonts to know how much do you think you can eat?"

"A couple of pieces."

"That all?"

"I think so."

"What part do you wont?"

"It don't matter."

She closed the door, but not all the way.

"I wont you to take some across the road to Tadpole and down home to your mama, you hear? This bag's Tadpole's and this bag's your mama's. And don't eat none on the way."

"Yes'm."

The screen door banged.

Cat came in with a plate with two pieces of chicken, a wing and a breast, and mashed potatoes and peas and cornbread.

"I can't eat all that much," I said.

"Well, try."

"I thought you just meant a couple of pieces of chicken."

"Well, you got to have stuff to go with it."

I sat up in bed and she put a cloth across my legs and the plate on the cloth.

"Thank you."

She went and sat down on the cedar chest.

"You ate?" I asked.

"Yeah, we awready ate. I looked in before and you was sleeping so hard I didn't wont to wake you."

"This is good."

"Thank you."

I ate for a few moments in silence, grease on my fingers. It was good to get real food again. My stomach had started caving in.

"You know, every time I cook fried chicken I think of that time Joe Hunn and me was married. My brother-in-law invited us over to a after-wedding supper. He wasn't married hisself so he cooked it up hisself. He started cooking it when we got there and then said dinner was ready and seem like to me it couldn't a been more than fifteen minutes, but I didn't say nothing. And then we sat down to eat, and I bit down on a piece and it had blood coming out of it. And Gus, that's his brother, was just saying, 'Good, ain't it?' and Joe was saying, 'Yeah.' I didn't know if Joe was crazy too or just didn't wont to 'fend him. But I put mine back down on the plate and said, 'I don't know about y'all, but this going back in the skillet.' So they let me put theirs back in the skillet too. If they'd have started laughing, I would have sweared it was a joke, but they didn't even crack a smile. Up to the day we separated, I never would let Joe Hunn fry me no chicken."

I laughed.

She said, "Here I am talking about that chicken and you trying to eat. I wasn't thinking I might upset your stomach."

"Naw, you didn't upset it."

"Well, I be in the house if you wont anything. You wont another piece of chicken?"

"Naw thanks, this is fine."

"I don't wont to worry you out of my own house. Call me when you through."

I said I would.

Her chicken was crisp, not bloody. I was thinking how I

never did like to get chicken ready to fry. Somebody else get it ready, then I'd fry it. Down home in the country, Mama used to wring the chickens' necks on a tree stump. I never would look. But when she got it all cut up and washed I'd fry it if she wanted me to. And that time that man sold me that fish and I put it on the tree stump and it started wiggling and jumped in the grass wiggling. I never would fry any more fish after that. Cousin Jesse said she could hear me all the way down the road screaming. She came up to see what was wrong, and then she took it down to her house and fried it for me, but when she brought it back I swear half the fish was gone. That was all right though. I know she wanted to feed them children with it.

Cat came back and took my plate.

"You sure you don't wont no more?"

"Yeah, I'm sure. I'm not sure what this'll do. It was good though. Thank you."

"You got those pills in case you need them, ain't you?"

"Yeah."

She took the plate out.

"She sleep?" It was Tad.

"Naw, she just got through eating."

"Mind if I go in?"

"You just seen her this morning."

"So?"

"Well, knock."

He knocked. I said, "Come in."

"How you feeling?" he asked.

"Okay."

"She treating you all right?"

"Yeah."

He stayed near the door. I told him to come on in.

"Naw, I just came to thank Cat for the chicken she sent over and thought I peep in and see how you was doing."

"I'm okay."

"Eating solid?"

"Yeah."

He went back out. I smiled.

I heard the front door close, then Cat came in.

"That nigger both'ring you?"

"Naw."

"Well, if he bothers you, tell me, and I won't let him come in here."

"You know how I feel."

"I know how you think you feel. But I ain't going into that no more . . . He brought Eddy Pace's group back."

"Did he?"

"Yeah."

"That's good."

"Be bout time for you to go over there if you was on your feet."

"Yeah, the after-supper show. Then go back in the evening. You know that."

She said nothing.

"He across the street?" I asked.

"Yeah, he's over there."

"He don't know I'm here I guess."

"I guess he don't."

"Pull that shade down, will you? And keep it down."

She pulled down the shade.

"All he wont to do is see you start back to work again. Know you on your feet. So he won't feel guilty."

"He got a lifetime of feeling guilty. I don't know how many lifetimes."

"It ain't right you to feel that way. I know he did wrong and you got to suffer the consequences. But he got consequences too."

"He can go out and give other women babies. What kind of consequences he got?"

"Consequences of loving you."

"Shit."

She came away from the window.

"It took you a long enough time to pull that shade down. If you wont him to know where I'm at, why don't you go over and tell him where I'm at."

"I don't care if he know or not, cause it ain't none of my business. But I guess I don't wont him to know. 'Cause if he don't cause trouble, *you* will. All he wonts to do is *see* you. But I don't know what you wont."

"All I wont is not to see that nigger. He can go to Kocomo for all I care."

"Yeah," she said.

"Yeah."

"It bother you though, don't it?" She grinned. "Trying to make it with Tadpole McCormick."

"I ain't trying. I have made it, for your information. What's wrong with Tadpole?"

"It ain't what's wrong with *him*, it's what's wrong with *you*. And he's too blind to see it. That's what's wrong with him. Every since he got that place and seen you singing there he's been in love with you. I don't doubt he *got* the place cause you was there. But you ain't paid him half a mind till this. It was always Mutt Thomas, Mutt Thomas, Mutt Thomas. I ain't even going to say nothing about the men, cause that ain't my place. But if you didn't have eyes to see *then*, you ain't got eyes to see *now*."

"I see what I need to see."

"Yeah, that's probably your trouble."

She turned her ass to me and went out.

"Fuck you," I said.

"You can't."

"Y'all hush." It was Lurene's voice. The screen door banged. "You know that woman's sick in there. You ought to wait."

"Sick or not sick they's things she's got to be told."

"Shhh."

Cat didn't shhh, she talked louder. "I know womens that's had it out been up by now. I don't even believe *that* no more. Cause they kept her down to St. Joseph long enough before she even got out."

"Well, she be up soon, you get evil enough," Lurene said. "Jeff be up in a little while. I got her down there drying the dishes, and I told her to come on up here. Well, I see you tomorrow morning then. I ain't hardly got no sleep and they going to have me standing up all night. You know Philip Lorry, the one I said work out there?"

"Yeah."

"I think he's started to get sweet on me, honey."

"Well, you need something to make working out there worth it."

"Yeah, don't I though. Well, I see you."

"Awright."

"Here she is. You be good now."

"Yes ma'am. Here the key."

"You lock it awright?"

"Yes ma'am."

"Awright, see y'all. Ain't you going to kiss me? . . . See you, Cat."

"Awright."

"If that nigger love me he wouldn't've throwed me down the steps," I called.

"What?" She came to the door.

"I said if that nigger loved me he wouldn't've throwed me down the steps."

"I know niggers love you do worse than that," she said.

"Miss Catherine, can I have another piece of chicken?" Jeffy said.

"Yeah, go on in and get it. Then you go on in there and sleep on the floor. You got to sleep on the floor tonight."

"She don't have to sleep on the floor, she can sleep in here with me," I said.

Cat said nothing. "Yeah, I said yeah," she told Jeffy.

When it was time to go to bed, Jeffy came in with a blanket. She started putting her blanket down on the throw rug on the floor.

"Honey, I said you could sleep up here with me. You don't have to sleep down there on the floor."

"Miss Catherine said for me to sleep down here."

"Well, I said you can sleep up here."

I turned back the sheets for her to get in. She left the blanket on the floor and came and got in the bed. I could smell fried chicken.

"You wiped your hands, didn't you?"

"Yeah."

"You yes ma'am your mama and yes ma'am Miss Catherine, how come you don't yes ma'am me?"

"You ain't nothing but twenty-five. I got a sister up in Detroit that's twenty-five. If I yes ma'am her she slap the shit out of me."

I said nothing.

"You settled?" I asked.

"Yeah."

I turned the light out.

"I seen your nigger pacing up and down over there."

"He ain't my nigger."

"Well, he used to be."

"Used to ain't now."

"You just scared of him, that's all."

"I like to see the day I was scared of Mutt Philmore Thomas."

"That his middle name?" she laughed.

I said nothing.

"I bet you be scared if I said I was going over there and tell him you was over here."

"You better not. I might not be that much older than you, honey, but I know how to slap shit too."

She said nothing. I thought I had hushed her, but then she said, "See if I don't."

"See if I don't tell your mama I seen you over there in Hawkins alley with that Logan boy."

"Naw, that was Luella you seen with Wayne. I was just watching."

"Well, that means you twice as nasty."

"I bet you was fucking before I was born. How much fucking you think you goin do now?"

It was my turn to say nothing.

"It don't mean you *can't*," I explained. "It just means . . ."

"I heard Mama talking bout women like that. Mess up their minds and then fuck up their pussy."

"You too young to talk like that."

"You too young to have it took out of you too. Tha's what mama said. She said, 'Ain't that awful and young as she is too. Jeff, now don't you go over there both'ring that woman neither, cause she got enough trouble.' "

"Nigger, get out of here."

"You said I could sleep with you."

"Then shut up and sleep. I told you I know how to slap shit too."

"You supposed to be sick. You ain't sick."

"I will be if you don't shut up."

"See if I don't tell that nigger of yours."

I started to slap her. I was going to if she said another word. She must have felt it because she didn't say nothing else. She started breathing hard, and then she must have been sleeping. I turned away from her and slept.

I was drowsy, but I felt her hands on my breasts. She was feeling all on me up around my breasts. I shot awake and knocked her out on the floor. It wasn't even daylight yet. It couldn't have been more than three o'clock. There was a smell of vomit in the room, like when you suck your thumb.

"Naw, bitch, you get the hell out of here," I said. "You take that goddamn blanket and get the goddamn hell out of here."

She was crying, not from anything I said, but she must have skinned her ass when she hit the floor. I turned on the light and she was sucking her arm and getting the blanket and crying. I kept calling her a goddamn bull, but I didn't like what else I was wondering. I was wondering how Cat Lawson got her to mind. Because that wasn't the kind of kid that would respect anybody on account of age.

Jeffy stumbled out the door.

"What's going on in nere?" I heard Cat say. "What you do?"

Jeffy didn't say nothing. Catherine came into the room, rubbing her eyes.

"What happen? What she do?" She sat down on the cedar chest, as if she already suspected what she did.

"She started feeling on me all up around here and I knocked her off on the floor," I said.

"I knowed she was like that, tha's why I told her to sleep in here on the floor."

"Well, you should've told me she was like that before and

I wouldn't have said she could come in here and sleep with me. Why in the hell didn't you tell me she was like that before?"

"I told her to sleep on the floor. You should've let her sleep on the floor."

"Well, she seem like she too young to be like that. How the hell was I suppose to know? I didn't wont the child sleeping on the damn floor and catch pneumonia."

"It's a hot night."

"Well. She can catch pneumonia of the asshole for all I care."

"Don't worry, she catch it."

I couldn't restrain myself. "What, you goin give it to her?"

She looked at me, drowsy, and hurt and angry.

"I told her to sleep on the floor," she said.

I said nothing. She got up as if waiting for me to say something, but I still said nothing. Before she left, she cut me a hard look. I gave up wondering. I knew if Jeffy had got in the bed with her and started pulling that shit, she would have knocked her on the floor too. She would have knocked her past the floor.

It wasn't so much how much fucking I was going to do now, I was thinking, but the consequences of that fucking. Shit. Cat telling me about the consequences of him loving me. Shit. What the hell did that mean? And her story. What about her and Joe Hunn? If I hadn't stopped wondering when she gave me that hard-as-steel look I would've guessed that story. Maybe it's just a man can't stand to have a woman as hard as he is. If he couldn't support her in money, he'd be wanting to support her in spirit. And what if I'd thrown Mutt Thomas down those stairs instead, and done away with the source of his sex, or inspiration, or whatever the hell it is for a man, what would he feel now? At least a woman's still got the hole. Look, nigger, I still got my hole. Finger-pop it. Your mama's a bitch, she was laid in a ditch. Naw, dropped you in one. And what they had to do in those days. I always get back to that. The tobacco fields or coffee ones. Hard because you have to be, but still those tender-eyed women and hands tender behind tobacco calluses with their men. Hurt you into tenderness finally. Is it more his fault than mine? Naw, when you start thinking that way. Naw, that nigger's to blame. What's bothering me? Great Gram, because I can't make generations. I remember everything you told me, Great Gram and Gram too and.

Good night, Ursa, baby. Good night, Irene. *Honey, I remember when you was a warm seed inside me, but I tried not to bruise you. Don't bruise any of your seeds. I won't, Mama. I never told you how Great Gram had Gram. She thought she had to go to the toilet, and then something told her not to go outside to the outhouse like she was going to, and then she squat down on the chamber pot. And then that's how she had your Gram, coming out in the slop jar. That's how we all begin, remember that. That's how we all begin. A mud ditch or a slop jar or hit the floor or the ground. It's all the same. But you got to make generations, you go on making them anyway. And when the ground and the sky open up to ask them that question that's going to be ask. They think it ain't going to be ask, but it's going to be ask. They have the evidence and give the verdict too. They think they hid everything. But they have the evidence and give the verdict too.* You said that, Mama. *I know I said it, and I'm going to keep saying it.*

"*Come in here.*"

I was out in the yard playing with the little boy from across the street. He'd bet me I didn't know how to play doctor. I bet him I did. We'd made a seesaw by putting a board across a tree stump. I lay across the board on my belly, and he raised up my dress. Mama saw us.

"Come in here. Go on home, Henry."

She jerked me in the back door by the arm, and slammed the door.

"Don't you know what that boy was doing? He was feeling up your asshole."

"I couldn't feel it."

"If I could see it, I know you could feel it."

"Mama, I couldn't feel it."

"Get on in here. Have people looking at you. What do you think, the neighbors ain't got eyes? What was he using?"

"I didn't feel nothing."

"Shut up. If I even think I see anything else, I'll beat you."

I bet you were fucking before I was born.

Before you was thought.

"Ursa, what makes your hair so long?"

"I got evil in me."

Corregidora's evil.

Ole man, he just kept rolling . . .

Cat knocked on the door. I said, "Come in." She came in, but stood near the door. It was the next day or, rather, later the same day. I was sitting up in bed.

Cat stood looking at me, then she said, "I'm sorry. I should have told you that was why I didn't want her in here."

"Tha's awright. It's all water under the bridge now."

"I still should have told you she was like that."

"I'd rather not talk about it."

"I just came in to see how many eggs you wont for breakfast."

"Two. As long as you don't send it by her."

"I won't. Anyway, her mama come and got her at seven."

"Does Lurene know?"

"I don't know what Lurene know. If she do, she haven't told me. They say Jeffy's daddy, something was wrong with him. But I didn't know him myself."

"You ask me, something must be wrong with all of 'em."

"Naw, don't get into that. Lurene's crazy about men as you are."

"Yeah, I heard her talking about some dude she got at work."

"Yeah, well, he help to make her day. Or I should say make her night."

I laughed. "Working night shift, he have to make her day."

"Well, I go fix breakfast."

"Cat, I don't think I can stay here."

"I make sure Jeffy don't even look at you while you here. I keep her outter here."

"It ain't that . . . I shouldn't stay here."

"You wont to be over there where that nigger is, don't you?"

"I expect to start back to work in a day or two," I said.

"Well, you stay here till you start back then."

"All right, a day or two," I said.

"Well, Tadpole be up in the air."

"What?"

"Hear you be singing again."

"I just hope I'm as good. It's been a long time."

"You be just as good."

"They didn't say anything about my throat. They didn't say it did anything to my throat."

"If it did they would've said something. You mean you ain't sing nothing since it happened?"

"Naw."

"Well, you sing for me tonight. Ain't use worrying for nothing."

I said nothing.

"I'll keep her out of here," she said, and went to fix the eggs.

"*Trouble in mind, I'm blue, but I won't be won't be blue always,*" I sang and stopped.

"Go on."

I was sitting up in bed. She was on the cedar chest. I went on and finished the song.

She smiled and clapped.

"It didn't sound like it used to," I said.

"Your voice sounds a little strained, that's all. But if I hadn't heard you before, I wouldn't notice anything. I'd still be moved. Maybe even moved more, because it sounds like you been through something. Before it was beautiful too, but you sound like you been through more now. You know what I mean?"

"I know what you mean, but it's still changed."

"Not for the worse. Like Ma, for instance, after all the alcohol and men, the strain made it better, because you could tell what she'd been through. You could hear what she'd been through."

"Well, I don't have to worry about the men," I said.

"That'd make you go through more, not having a man," she said, and looked as if she'd wished she hadn't said it.

I went on as if I hadn't heard it. "Well, we'll see when I go on tomorrow."

"Tomorrow?"

"Well, okay, day after tomorrow."

"Okay. And first night make it just supper or evening, but not both. I'll speak to Tad if you don't."

"I don't think he'd let me sing both anyway."

"Naw, he wouldn't."

"You sure it's okay?"

"It's more than okay."

She left me. I lay back and tried to sleep, but couldn't. I started humming the part about taking my rocking chair down by the river and rocking my blues away. What she said about the voice being better because it tells what you've been through. Consequences. It seems as if you're not singing the past, you're humming it. Consequences of what? Shit, we're all consequences of something. Stained with another's past as well as our own. Their past in my blood. I'm a blood. *Are you mine, Ursa, or theirs?* What he would ask. What would I ask now? Do you want to see me? Naw, I don't want to see you, I want to screw you. When he wanted to make up with me he'd always ask if I remembered such and such a thing. Do you remember that time we . . . Hell, yes, I remember. Blues songs and stroking your neck and laughter and sighs inside knees that made us hold each other tighter. When he got back from work he'd ask me to rub his thighs. Do you feel how tight the muscles are? Yes. My hand on his belly then. The mark of his birth. I'd tell him, I have a birthmark between my legs. That would make him laugh. But it's your fault all my seeds are wounded forever. No warm ones, only bruised ones, not even bruised ones. No seeds. Let me in between your legs. It ain't a pussy down there, it's a whole world.

Talking about *his* pussy. Asking me to let him see his pussy. Let me feel my pussy. The center of a woman's being. Is it? No seeds. Is that what snaps away my music, a harp string broken, guitar string, string of my banjo belly. Strain in my voice. Yes, I remember your hands on my ass. Your damn hands on my ass. That vomity feeling when they squeezed my womb out. Is that the way you treat someone you love? Even my clenched fists couldn't stop the fall. That old man still howls inside me. You asked me how did I get to be so beautiful. It wasn't *him*. No, not Corregidora. And my spirit, you said, like knives dancing. My veins are centuries meeting. You scratched behind my ear and drew blood and then kissed where you scratched. You can't kiss where you scratched anymore. No, anyway, I don't believe what Cat said your reasons are. You don't treat love that way. When you came and heard my music you requested songs, and then when you had me alone, you requested more than my songs. I can still feel your fucking inside me. If it wasn't for your fucking I. When do you sing the blues? Every time I ever want to cry, I sing the blues. Or would there be glasses of tears? Yes, there would be spilled glasses. I came to you, open and wounded. And you said, Sing for me, goddamn it, sing. Your plate was stained with flies, and you kept requesting songs. I sang to you out of my whole body.

"Urs, do you remember?"

"Yes, I remember. Who told you I was here?"

"The girl did."

"I thought she would, the little bitch."

"If she hadn't, I wouldn't have found you."

"You never lost me."

The shit you can dream. I struggled out of sleep. My eyes felt as tight as fists, but they opened. Light came in through the yellow shade. The shit you can dream. They say it's what you really feel, but it ain't what you really feel.

I wondered if Cat was up. I got up and put on my robe. But I didn't want to see that Jeffy if she was out there, so I sat down on the cedar chest and waited. I still felt sleepy, but I knew I couldn't sleep. I held my arms around my belly. Then I got up and opened the door and went out in the living room. Jeffy wasn't there. I had expected to see her in there. The clock on the mantelpiece said it was close to five o'clock. I wrapped my robe around me and stood in the living room. Then I heard Cat talking.

"If you bother her again I'll give you a fist to fuck."

"I ain't going to bother her again."

"I said if you do you got my fist to fuck."

Then there was silence.

"I could've told you she wouldn't."

"What? You ask her?"

There was a loud slap, and then low crying.

"Laugh now."

"Please, Miss Catherine."

"I said, 'Laugh now.'"

Low crying.

"I didn't go in there to do it. I must've did it in my sleep."

"Shit if you did."

Silence.

"Shit."

"I grab the shit out of you, you little nigger."

"Shit."

"Hush."

I had eased back to the door and by the time the "hush" came, I'd stepped back into the bedroom.

"What is it?"

"Hush."

Silence.

I sat on the cedar chest with my robe open, then I got dressed. I think if Cat or Jeffy had come into the room then, I would've got evil. I would have got right evil. It wasn't until years later that I realized it might have been because of my own fears, the things I'd thought about in the hospital, my own worries about what being with a man would be like again, and whether I really had the nerve to try. But then I just felt evil.

I left the boxes at the foot of the bed. I put my bed-clothes and cosmetics in a sack and went out the door and across the street. I'd send Tadpole for the boxes later. The front door was locked and I went up the back-stairs and knocked on the door. It took him a long time to come.

"Ursa, baby, what you doing over here? You awright?"

"I want to come in," I said.

I must have been looking hateful. He asked me what was wrong.

"A lot of shit," I said. He'd been sleeping on the bed where I'd been sleeping when I was there. I went and sat down at the foot of the bed. He kept standing, looking at me.

"What do you mean?"

"Well, you know Jeffy stay over there."

"Yeah."

I didn't say what I was going to. "She just stay over there. I'm taking up Jeffy's space."

"That ain't why you here," he said.

I started to tell him, but didn't. I only told him about Jeffy in the bed, feeling all on my breasts. I didn't tell him what I'd overheard. I didn't tell him what Cat was. I didn't tell him why I'd really left.

"She should have told me Jeffy was like that before, and I wouldn't have said she could come in and sleep with me.

Cat knew she was like that, that's why she told her to sleep on the floor."

"She could have told her to sleep on the couch," Tadpole said.

"Cat don't allow nobody to sleep on the couch, because she says it's the only decent thing she got and she wonts to keep it decent."

"And you ain't going back over there?"

"Naw."

"I guess you wont me to go over there and get your stuff for you?"

"Little later. If you don't mind."

He said nothing.

"She seem like she too young to be like that," I said.

"Well, they start off young."

He came over to the bed and sat down.

"Sit closer to me," he said.

I sat closer.

He pulled me closer.

"Does it hurt?"

"Yes, a little."

"Did they say you could do it?"

"Yes, we can do it."

"How does it feel now?"

"Go on."

"How did you sleep?" Tad asked.

I said nothing. I put my cheek against his chest. He said it was time for him to go down and open up. I watched him rise.

After a while I got up.

"I thought you'd still sleep," he said, when he came back. I'd made the bed, but hadn't folded it back to be a couch.

"I'll just rest today," I said. "I want to start work this evening."

"Do you think you're ready? I don't think you're ready."

"I feel like it. The doctor said whenever I felt like it."

"After two weeks, he said."

"I feel like it now. I want to, Tad."

"No more than an hour, and only one show."

"The evening one."

"Okay. And I'll have them get a chair for you."

"I never sat down singing."

"Well, tonight you will."

"No, not tonight either."

"If you seem tired or anything I'll just tell them the show's over."

"I won't. I'll be okay."

"You rest a lot then." He unmade the bed.

I looked at him.

"I'll feel better if you rest a lot," he said, and went back downstairs.

I'd put on my robe but hadn't dressed. I sat back down on the bed. Then I started singing about trouble in mind. Still the new voice. The one Cat said you could hear what I'd been through in. I tried not to think about the rest of what I'd heard Cat say.

They call it the devil blues. It ride your back. It devil you. I bit my lip singing. I troubled my mind, took my rocker down by the river again. It was as if I wanted them to see what he'd done, hear it. All those blues feelings. That time I asked him to try to understand my feeling ways. That's what I called it. My feeling ways. My voice felt like it was screaming. What do they say about pleasure mixed in the pain? That's the way it always was with him. The pleasure somehow greater than the pain. My voice screaming for him to take me. And when he would, I'd draw him down into the bottom of my eyes. They watched me. I felt as if they could see my feelings somewhere in the bottom of my eyes.

I saw Mutt's cousin Jimmy come in while I was singing about trouble. He sat down at a table. I was singing my last two songs. Singing and trying not to see the face outside the window, troubling my eyes. When I finished, Jim came up to me. "Jimmy, how are you?" I asked. He asked me to come have a drink with him. I nodded and went over with him and sat down. I saw Tadpole watching us, but I didn't look back at Tadpole. I didn't look at the man outside the window.

"Do it trouble you me in here?" Jim asked.

"Why should it? You ain't him."

"You did fine. It's good to see you back."

I said nothing. Then I said, "Tell him to go away, Jim."

"He worries."

"Tell him I'm all right, and he can go away."

"He got the papers from your lawyer and signed them. He said if that's what you wont."

"Yes."

"It ain't what he wonts."

"I never did know what he wonted."

"He just wont you to come outside and say something to him."

"I already cussed him out. In the hospital I cussed him out. I thought everybody I seen was him and I cussed everybody I seen out. I kept looking up cussing everybody."

"He said he go away. He just wont you to come out and say something to him before he go away."

"I'm not going out there and say nothing to him, Jim."

He said nothing. He sipped his drink.

"I guess he be going away without it then."

"Don't do that, Jim. Don't try to draw my pity. It ain't there."

"It's there."

"What do you mean?"

"It's there. It's just turned all inside."

I wanted to slap him but didn't.

"I never have pitied myself and never will," I said.

"You pitied yourself when you left Bracktown and came to the city and you been pitying yourself ever since."

"Shit. Don't try to make it easy for him, Jim. I never thought of you that way."

"You never thought of me anyway," he said. He took another sip.

I watched him, but said nothing.

"What man was you singing to now?" he asked.

"What?"

"Once you told me that when you sang you always had to pick out a man to sing to. And when Mutt started coming in, you kept picking out him to sing to. And then when y'all was married, you had your man to sing to. You said that you felt that the others only listened, but that he heard you."

I said nothing. Then, "Don't worry about it."

"I ain't."

"Well, don't."

"I think there's your old man."

"What?"

"Tadpole Mac-I-want-my-woman-back giving me the evil eye. I think he wants you." He finished his drink and stood up.

I kept looking at him. I wouldn't look at the window, or at Tadpole, behind the bar.

"Thank you," he said.

"For what?"

"I enjoyed the music."

I rolled my eyes at him, but looked back at him.

"He told me to ask you something. He said you know what it meant."

"Ask me what?"

"What's a husband for?"

I took my eyes off him.

"It'll keep hurting, Urs."

I kept my eyes off him. He started towards the door.

"Him or me?" I called.

He went out. When I looked to see if Mutt was still there, he wasn't.

Tadpole came from behind the bar.

"You better get upstairs," he said.

He didn't ask what Jim wanted. I thought he would, but he didn't.

I got up, tired, but trying not to show it.

"You coming up?" I asked.

"I got to close up first. I be up. Do you want me to take you up?"

"Naw."

Tad went back to the bar. I saw men watching me as I walked across the room.

I went upstairs and undressed, put on my robe, but didn't get in bed.

"*Songs are devils. It's your own destruction you're singing. The voice is a devil.*"

"*Naw, Mama. You don't understand. Where did you get that?*"

"*Unless your voice is raised up to the glory of God.*"

"*I don't know where you got that.*"

But still I'll sing as you talked it, your voice humming,

sing about the Portuguese who fingered your genitals. His pussy. "The Portuguese who bought slaves paid attention only to the genitals." Slapped you across the cunt till it was bluer than black. Concubine daughter.

"Where did you get those songs? That's devil's music."

"I got them from you."

"I didn't hear the words."

Then let me give witness the only way I can. I'll make a fetus out of grounds of coffee to rub inside my eyes. When it's time to give witness, I'll make a fetus out of grounds of coffee. I'll stain their hands.

Everything said in the beginning must be said better than in the beginning.

I didn't know what time it was when Tadpole came up.

"I thought you'd be in bed."

"Naw."

"Thank you for waiting for me."

I said nothing. He got undressed and came and sat beside me.

"You were beautiful, honey," he said. His hand went under my robe, stroking my shoulder.

"I know what they must have been saying about my voice," I said.

He shook his head. "It sounded like it had sweat in it. Like you were pulling everything out of yourself. You were beautiful, sweet."

"Did you see him?"

"Yeah, I saw him."

"I thought he might try to get in."

"Naw, he wasn't going to try to do that."

He still didn't ask me what Jim wanted. I was glad. His hands were gentle hard on my belly, then stroking my thighs.

"I love you," he said.

I said nothing. I was thinking I'd only wanted him to love me without saying anything about it. Cat had told me enough. I was grateful he didn't ask me the same question.

"What did you and Jim talk about?" he asked finally.

"He wanted me to come out and talk. Mutt did."

"And you didn't."

"He says Mutt's released me."

He was stroking my thigh.

"You heard what I said," he said.

"Yes."

"I want you to be my wife."

I nodded, but he wasn't looking.

"Did you hear what I said?"

"Yes. I mean, yes I'll marry you."

He drew me into bed.

"Are you relaxed now?" he asked.

I said yes I was relaxed now. I started to tell him Jim said Mutt wasn't coming back, but I didn't. Tadpole got between my legs.

"*What's a husband for?*"

"*Somebody to give your piece of ass to.*"

"*Mutt, just suppose something was in there when they took it out? What would you feel then?*"

"*Was something in there?*"

"*Just suppose.*"

"*Don't make any promises you can't keep.*"

". . . They would bend down with their fingers feeling up your pussy."

"*You don't care if you ever see me again, do you?*"

"*Naw, I don't care.*"

"What do Mutt do?"

"He works in tobacco."

"What do you remember?"

"I could feel your thing. I could smell you in my nostrils."

What do blues do for you?

It helps me to explain what I can't explain.

I was already awake when he woke up. He looked over at me and rubbed under my eyes.

"You dark under your eyes," he said.

"That's mascara."

"Aw."

He touched my cheek.

"Do you know what your eyes do?"

"No."

"They make a man feel like he wants to climb inside them."

Fall to the bottom of my eyes. What will you do there?

"Can I do the supper show tonight?" I asked.

"Not unless you check with Dr. Stevens first."

"He said I should gradually increase time."

"Not your kind of gradual. You saw the chair I had sitting there for you."

"Yeah, I saw it."

"I think you ought to go tell Dr. Stevens you working awready."

"I feel like it."

"I still think you should go over there. I'll drive you over there as soon as I get things started and Sal gets here. Otherwise, I won't feel right."

I said okay I'd go.

"You pushed it, didn't you? Started to work now."

"I had to."

"How do you feel?"

"I'm all right."

"Well, the nurse'll take care of you. I'll be in in a minute."

I went into the examining room and undressed and got up on the table. The doctor came in. He started feeling my belly, feeling places and asking me if it hurt. I kept saying Naw.

"Did you get tired out last night?" he asked.

I said Naw.

"Well, there doesn't seem to be anything wrong. Any more nausea?"

"Naw."

"Well, get dressed. Stop back and see me before you leave."

I got dressed and went back into the doctor's office.

"I'm going to put you on some iron pills anyway."

He wrote out a prescription.

"Have you started back having sexual relations yet?"

"Yes, why? Is there something wrong with it?"

"No, there's nothing wrong with it," he said. "But just don't push it either."

He handed me the prescription.

"I don't think you need to come back for, say, three weeks. And we'll see how the work's going. Don't push your time too much. Like I said before. A little bit every night. I'd say don't push it more than a half an hour extra each time."

"I wanted to do the supper show."

"Forty-five minutes, then, each show. Then that'd give you time to rest in between."

I thanked him and started out.

"Make an appointment with the nurse, will you?"

"Okay."

I made an appointment, and then Tad and I went outside.

"What did he say?"

"He said there was nothing wrong with me. He wants me to get these iron pills."

Tad took the prescription and said he'd stop and get it filled on the way home.

I sang the supper show. There was no Mutt in the window. And in the evening, there was no Mutt. But when I got to the last couple of songs, Jim came in and sat down. When I finished I went over to the table.

"Mutt send you here to watch me?" I asked.

"I got just as much right to be here as anybody else," he said. He'd ordered a beer and was drinking.

"It's about closing time," I said.

"I just come in here to get me a little beer," he said. "I ain't studying you or Mutt."

"He left me when he throwed me down those steps. I didn't leave him." I hadn't sit down. I was standing, speaking low so I wouldn't draw attention.

"I don't know what's wrong with you, woman," he said loud. People turned and looked.

I was embarrassed.

"Okay, Jim," I said, again low. I could feel my eyebrows pulling together. "You got just as much right to be here as anybody, you hear."

"You trying to get dangerous?"

"Naw, I'm not trying to get dangerous," I said. I walked away.

When I got upstairs, Tadpole came in after me.

"What's that about?"

"He's just being a bastard."

"Wont me to bar *him* too?"

I didn't like the way he said it. I looked at him.

"Naw, he's got just as much right to be here as anybody,"
I said.

"He bothering you about Mutt?"

"Naw, he didn't say nothing about Mutt."

"I'll let you turn in," he said.

"What if I'd said yes?"

"I'd go ask him what right's he got to be here."

I didn't know if he were joking or not. He wasn't smiling.
He went back downstairs.

I took one of my iron pills. I swallowed it and closed my
eyes. I wanted a song that would touch me, touch my life
and theirs. A Portuguese song, but not a Portuguese song.
A new world song. A song branded with the new world. I
thought of the girl who had to sleep with her master and
mistress. Her father, the master. Her daughter's father. The
father of her daughter's daughter. How many generations?
Days that were pages of hysteria. Their survival depended
on suppressed hysteria. She went and got her daughter,
womb swollen with the child of her own father. How many
generations had to bow to his genital fantasies? They were
fishermen and planters. And you with the coffee-bean face,
what were you? You were sacrificed. They knew you only
by the signs of your sex. They touched you as if you were
magic. They ate your genitals. And you, Grandmama, the
first mulatto daughter, when did you begin to feel yourself
in your nostrils? And, Mama, when did you smell your body
with your hands?

"Was your mama mulatto?" Mutt asked once.

"I'm darker than her."

"Did that question make you mad?"

"No."

"You look mad."

"I'm not. It's a long story. Too long for now."

"Will you tell me sometime?"

"Yes."

I never really told him. I gave him only pieces. A few more pieces than I'd given Tadpole, but still pieces.

"Your pussy's a little gold piece, ain't it, Urs? My little gold piece."

"Yes."

"Ursa, I'm worried about you, you so dark under your eyes."

He tried to tell me I was working too hard, wasn't getting enough sleep, said that was another reason he wanted me to stop working at Happy's—besides the men. I told him my eyes weren't dark. I told him it was just the mascara. But then he tried to rub it off, and it wouldn't come off.

"Why did you lie, baby?"

And that time he had his cousin take a picture of me and him, and I kept staring at the picture.

He said, "We look good, don't we, honey?"

I got so embarrassed because it was me I was looking at, not *us*. I handed him back the picture and he put it on the mirror. But when he wasn't there I'd come by the bureau and just look at it. I'd never look when Mutt was home. But I knew why I was looking. Because I realized for the first time I had what all those women had. I'd always thought I was different. *Their* daughter, but somehow different. Maybe less Corregidora. I don't know. But when I saw that picture, I knew I had it. What my mother and my mother's mother before her had. The mulatto women. Great Gram was the coffee-bean woman, but the rest of us . . . But I *am* different now, I was thinking. I have everything they had, except the generations. I can't make generations. And even if I still had my womb, even if the first baby *had* come—what would I have done then? Would I have kept it up? Would I have been like *her*, or *them*?

"Did they have any other children?" I'd asked Mama once when they weren't there. I'd been afraid to ask when they were there, because I'd asked Great Gram once when I was real small if Grandmama had any brothers or sisters, and she'd given me this real hateful look.

Mama looked at me for a moment, at first like she wasn't going to answer, then she said, "I think there was some boys. I think they told me there was some boys, but Corregidora sold the boys off."

"Why?"

"Don't ask *them* that. The only reason I'm telling you is so you won't ask them."

"Ursa, wake up Ursa, baby."

He was stroking my hair.

"You must have been having a nightmare."

He got into bed with me, stroking my hair.

"Was it the old man again?"

"Yes."

He stroked my hair. "I'll stay with you," he said.

My voice was dancing, slow and blue, my voice was dancing, but I was saying nothing. I dreamed with my eyes open. All the Corregidora women with narrow waists and high cheekbones and wide hips. All the Corregidora women dancing. And he wanted me. He grabbed my waist.

"Ain't even took my name. You Corregidora's, ain't you? Ain't even took my name. You ain't my woman."

"You had a bad night, didn't you?"

"Yes."

"Get their devils off your back. Not yours, *theirs.*"

I said nothing. I pretended I didn't know what he meant.

Tadpole arranged things with the justice of the peace and we were married. Tadpole wanted Cat Lawson to be the witness. I said Naw, then I finally conceded, because I couldn't tell him why not. I didn't know how it would be, because I was finding it difficult to even say anything to her. And I felt that she must have suspected why I left. I hadn't been over there since the morning I'd walked out, and she hadn't been to visit me. She scarcely said anything before the ceremony, and then when we were driving back, she didn't say a word.

"Cat got your tongue?" Tadpole asked.

"Yeah, I got my own tongue," she said. She was sitting on the side by the window. I was in the middle.

"You happy for us, ain't you?" he asked.

"You know I wish you all the happiness in the world," Cat said.

I didn't say anything.

When we got home, Cat said, "You can just drop me off here."

"You coming in and have a drink with us, ain't you?"

"Naw, Tadpole, it's too early in the day for me."

"Since when?"

Cat looked at me, but I said nothing.

"Come on," Tad said.

"Well, awright. I just have a nip though."

We got out of the car and went inside. Tadpole had Sal's husband, Thedo, take over at the bar while we were gone. His real name was Theodore, but everybody called him Thedo.

"Thedo, some champagne," said Tadpole.

"I just have some plain old Kentucky bourbon myself," said Cat.

"Naw, I got a bottle down there especially for the occasion," said Tadpole. "Thedo."

Thedo got out the champagne and poured.

"If I get a bellyache it's y'all's fault."

"This is delicate stuff," said Tadpole.

"Well, my stomach ain't been used to delicate."

Tadpole laughed. I drank. Then I said, "Honey, I think I'm going upstairs. I'm a little tired."

"Awright, baby," he said, frowning.

Cat was looking at me, but I didn't look at her.

"So long, Cat," I said, without looking at her, to make it sound right.

"Sure, see you around," Cat said.

I got up from the stool.

"All women just married act funny?" I heard Tad ask.

"Yeah," Cat answered.

It was a short time after I came up that there was a knock on the door. I knew who it was before she opened.

"Can I come in?" she asked.

"You already are," I said. I was sitting on the bed, getting out of my stockings. I laid them on the chair, then I took them off the chair, and put them on the bed beside me. Cat came in and sat down in the chair. I didn't look up at her at first. Then I looked up at her. She was looking at me calmly, but I could tell she was hurt. I was hurt too. She was sweaty from drinking.

"You look flushed," I said.

She said nothing. Then she said, "I heard you in there that morning." Her voice was steadier than I thought it might be, all the time I'd imagined such a talk.

"Did you?" I said. I had nothing else to say.

"It was easier not to let you know I heard you then," she said.

I said nothing this time.

"I want you to know I heard you now."

"What does it matter?" I asked.

"Don't make me feel clumsier than I already do," she said.

"I didn't know you felt that way," I said coolly now.

She said nothing.

"Do you feel good treating me this way?" she asked.

"No, I don't feel good about any of it," I said.

There was silence. She sat looking at me. I'd stopped looking at her again. I could feel her flutter as if she wanted to say something, but she didn't. I wouldn't make it easy. I waited.

Then she said finally, "You don't know what it's like to feel foolish all day in a white woman's kitchen and then have to come home and feel foolish in the bed at night with your man. I wouldn't a mind the other so much if I didn't have to feel like a fool in the bed with my man. You don't know what that means, do you?"

I said nothing. She was crying but they were dry tears.

"I wanted to be able to come home to my own bed and not feel foolish. You don't know what it feels like."

She was looking at me, expecting something. She wanted me to tell her that I knew what it was like, but I wouldn't tell her. Yes, I know what it feels like. I remembered how his shoulders felt when he was going inside me and I had my hands on his shoulders, but I also remembered that night I was exhausted with wanting and I waited but he didn't turn toward me and I kept waiting and wanting him and I got close to him up against his back but he still wouldn't turn to me and then I lay on my back and tried hard to sleep and I finally slept and in the morning I waited and still he didn't and I thought in the morning he would but he didn't and I waited but the clock got him up and he went off to work and I lay there still waiting. I was no longer even angry with waiting. I just lay there saying don't make me use my fingers, and then I got up too. Yes, I could tell her what it feels like. *Do I have to wait until in the morning? Don't punish me this way. What's a husband for? Don't you feel like a man?* And wanting to cry and not wanting him to see me and turning over against the wall until sweat came out of my eyes but never wanting him to hear me cry.

"I didn't wont to be a fool in front of them and then have to come home and be a fool with him too. Couldn't even get in my own bed and not be a fool and have him making me feel like a fool too."

Two swollen plums for eyes. What are you doing to the girl? I wanted to ask. What about when it comes her time? Do you know what *I* mean? But she was telling me about Mr. and Mrs. Thomas Hirshorn and something that happened in the kitchen. She was a young woman, about my age. She lived in during the week and every morning at six o'clock she had to get up and get Mr. Hirshorn's breakfast because he was the supervisor in a plant, and his wife stayed in the bed sleeping. He always waited till she called him, but one morning he was sitting at the table while she was fixing coffee. "You pretty, Catherine, you know that? You pretty, Catherine. A lot of you nigger women is pretty." She kept thinking he was drunk, and wished he'd stayed in the room with his wife till she called him like she always did. But he kept sitting, thumping on the table, watching her, her bare arms in a housedress. "You ought to let me watch you straighten your hair sometime. Beatrice said you were in there straightening your hair." She was saying nothing and then when she'd got the can of coffee grounds down and was opening it to pour in the pot, he was behind her, touching her arm, and she dropped the can, and it banged and rolled across the kitchen floor spilling grains. He jumped back, and she was stooping trying to clean it up when his wife came in. "What happened, Tom?"

"That clumsy nigger. I won't have time to eat breakfast this morning, sweetheart."

While she was bending, she could see him bending to kiss his wife's mouth, then he went out the kitchen door, stepping over coffee grounds.

"You made a mess," his wife said, and went back to bed.

"I wanted to come back home to my own bed and not be made a fool of. You know what I mean?"

I said nothing. I waited for her to calm down. She kept watching me. I waited till the trembling stopped. I must have waited fifteen minutes.

"You over your hysteria now?" I asked.

"Don't judge me," she said.

"I won't judge you." I looked at her.

She was waiting for an embrace that I refused to give, then she stood up.

"Things pass over you like that," she said.

I didn't know what she meant, but didn't ask. She kept looking at me. I wouldn't look up at her.

"This means the end of it, I suppose."

"Whatever you feel it means," I said.

"I guess you didn't tell *him*."

"No."

"You won't, will you?"

I said nothing.

She waited a moment, then she said, "They never let you live it down." She went out.

"Yes, if you understood me, Mama, you'd see I was trying to explain it, in blues, without words, the explanation some-where behind the words. To explain what will always be there. Soot crying out of my eyes." O Mister who come to

my house You do not come to visit You do not come to see
me to visit You come to hear me sing with my thighs You
come to see me open my door and sing with my thighs
Perhaps you watch me when I am sleeping I don't know if
you watch me when I am sleeping. Who are you? I am the
daughter of the daughter of the daughter of Ursa of cur-
rents, steel wool and electric wire for hair.

While mama be sleeping, the ole man he crawl into bed
While mama be sleeping, the old man he crawl into bed
When mama have wake up, he shaking his nasty ole
head

Don't come here to my house, don't come here to my
house I said
Don't come here to my house, don't come here to my
house I said
Fore you get any this booty, you gon have to lay down
dead
Fore you get any this booty, you gon have to lay down
dead

". . . There were two alternatives, you either took one or
you didn't. And if you didn't you had to suffer the conse-
quences of not taking it. There was a woman over on the
next plantation. The master shipped her husband out of
bed and got in the bed with her and just as soon as he was
getting ready to go in her she cut off his thing with a razor
she had hid under the pillow and he bled to death, and
then the next day they came and got her and her husband.
They cut off her husband's penis and stuffed it in her
mouth, and then they hanged her. They let him bleed to
death. They made her watch and then they hanged her."

I got out of my wedding suit and was sitting on the
couch/bed in my slip when Tadpole came in.

"Y'all women sho act funny at wedding time," he said. He was excited with drink. He sat down and held me around the waist and kissed me. I'd been sitting stiffly but relaxed and returned the kiss. He squeezed my breasts.

"That hurt?"

"Naw."

"It hurts some women."

"It doesn't hurt me," I said.

I sat there, letting him hold me around the waist. I was saying nothing.

"I told Thedo to stay on the rest of the day. I thought maybe you might wont to drive down to Midway or over to Versailles or something."

"Naw."

"Aw, that's right, you said you was tired. You been taking those iron pills the doctor give you?"

"Yeah. I'm all right now though. I just felt a little tired. But I'm all right."

"You want to do anything? I'll take you somewhere else for dinner tonight. Maybe over to the Spider or something."

"I thought I'd be singing the supper show tonight."

"I won't have you working on your wedding day."

"You won't start that too, will you?"

"Start what?"

"Nothing. It's not the working. I'd like to sing for you."

"Sing for me here," he said. He unbuckled his pants and lay down on the bed. I sang for him, then we made love.

II

Sal Cooper and I had never been friends. She worked during the day and would leave during the supper show, so that we weren't there more than two hours together. But even during that time she'd always managed to avoid me. I tried to be friendly at first, but she didn't act friendly back, and I've always been the kind of person that when I see somebody don't want to be bothered with me, I don't be bothered with them. So it surprised me when she came over and said something to me. And when people started changing in their feelings toward me, I wasn't one to begrudge them. I didn't even suspect why she was being nice *then*, though now, when I think back on it and what she told me then, I think I know why. I'd married Tadpole, and Tadpole was dark like she was.

"How was the ceremony?" she asked, sitting down. She hadn't said anything when we came back from the wedding. She waited a couple of days before she said anything.

"It was nice," I said. I smiled.

She didn't return the smile but she had a pleasant look on her face. It was two o'clock in the afternoon, the time of day when there's not much business, and she was taking her break. I'd come downstairs because it was so hot upstairs, and I was tired of staying up there. We just sat there saying nothing. She was having a Coke. I had a beer.

"You know every since I first laid eyes on you I thought you was one of my long-lost relatives. I can't help it, I just kept feeling that you kin to me. You know, I'm a spiritualist. I believe in things like that."

I kept looking at her. I didn't know what she was talking about.

"I reckon you think I'm crazy, don't you?"

"No," I said, but I wasn't sure what I thought.

She sat silent a moment. I didn't say anything either.

Then she explained, "My mother came out the darkest, and so they wouldn't claim her. I don't know who they are. I don't even know what they look like. Mama probably wouldn't even know them now. She think they up in New York somewhere now though, passing. I don't know, but when I first saw you, I had that feeling."

"I couldn't pass," I said. I had to say something. I felt resentful, and a little angry because she was saying those things to me.

"I don't mean passing white. I mean passing for Spanish or something, you know. Like Cole Bean getting in the front door down at the Strand that time."

I started to say I didn't know, but I nodded.

"Come over here, baby."

I went over to the car. He was a black man but he had two white girls in the back seat. One of them was barefooted and had her legs up on the seat. Another black man was sitting in front, leaning across the seat looking at me. The other man was out of the car, smiling, showing his gold tooth.

"What's your name, baby?"

"Ursa."

"My name's Urban, Urban Jones. They both kind of sound alike, don't they. The Ur."

I nodded.

"What are you?" he asked.

"I'm an American."

"I know you a American," he said. "But what nationality. You Spanish?"

"Naw."

"You look like you Spanish. Where you from?"

"Kentucky."

"Maybe that's why you talk like that. What's your address? I want to come and see you."

I said nothing.

"What's wrong?"

"Nothing."

"Something's wrong, sweetheart. Your boyfriend wouldn't like it?"

I didn't have a boyfriend, but I said, "Naw."

"Well, he don't have to know."

"He'd have to know," I said.

"Well, I thought maybe I could take you out to dinner or something."

"No."

"Well, you pretty."

I smiled and said I had to go.

"Can I drop you somewhere?"

"Naw, I got to meet somebody."

"Your boyfriend?"

"Yeah," I lied.

He frowned, "Well, take it easy, honey." He got back in the car and drove off. I kept walking. That was the summer Mama had taken me up to Detroit. I was seventeen, but everybody said I looked older than I was.

"Do you know what you are?"

"What?"

"What all you got in you. I know you got something else in you that funny name you got."

I said I didn't know.

She kept looking at me. I could tell she wanted to confess something else, and to me. I took a sip of beer and waited.

"My mother married a light man so that her children could have light skin and good hair. But look what happened."

I frowned. We sat there saying nothing again.

"... *They burned all the documents, Ursa, but they didn't burn what they put in their minds. We got to burn out what they put in our minds, like you burn out a wound. Except we got to keep what we need to bear witness. That scar that's left to bear witness. We got to keep it as visible as our blood.*"

"I didn't bother you, did I?" Sal asked.

"Naw, you didn't bother me," I said. I didn't smile this time, but she was still looking at me as if she liked me for the first time. "No, I'm not bothered," I repeated.

"Cat thinks you're beautiful," she said, smiling, showing two gold teeth.

I said nothing.

"Cat ain't been around in a month of Sundays, have she?"

"Naw, she ain't been around," I said.

A man and a woman entered.

"I better go take care of these people," Sal said. She got up.

"You red-headed heifer." That's what that woman down in Bracktown called me. I wasn't even studying her man. He looked at me, I didn't look at him.

I sat there a moment, finishing my beer, then went back upstairs to take a nap before the supper show.

The last time I was in Bracktown, I went to the Baptist church with Mama.

"Who's that? Some new bitch from out of town going be trying to take everybody's husband away from them?" somebody asked.

"Naw, that's Ursa, that's my baby."

"Is that little Ursa? She growed up."

"Yeah, she have."

The church supper.

"Can I help you to some potato salad?" he asked me.

I let him help me to some. I didn't see she was with him but she kept watching. Then when he wasn't there, she eased over. "You red-headed heifer." Then when I was just walking down the street minding my own business, these two women in a car. "You red-headed heifer." I didn't stay long back in Bracktown. Just to see how folks was.

I'd slept for an hour when Tadpole came in. He was walking softly trying not to awake me, but I was already awake.

"Aw, I thought you was sleep," he said when he saw my eyes open.

"Naw."

"I was just over to Cat's," he said. "She said something crazy about going back to Versailles cause her roots was there. I told her her roots was wherever she take them. She said naw your roots are where you was born and you can't pull them up, the only thing you can do is cut yourself away from them but they still be there."

"Well, you can't sew yourself back onto them," I said. Then I thought that seemed a plea for her staying, but I didn't care.

"I finally told her to do whichever way she feel it," he said. "I had to tell her something. She act like she was looking for my approval or something. I just told her to do it the way she feel it. I told her she got all her customers here though."

"What did she say?"

"She said she try to get customers there too, and if she can't, then she do whatever she have to."

I said nothing.

"I told her to take care of herself. You going over there to see her before she leave, ain't you?"

"Yeah," I said, but I knew I wasn't going over there. I asked him when was she leaving. He said probably tomorrow morning.

"I said we be coming down to see her, but she said she didn't know where she was going to live yet. That's funny, ain't it?"

I said it was funny.

I went in to take a bath and get ready for the supper show.

Jim would still come in sometimes to have a beer, but now I didn't say nothing to him and he didn't say nothing to me. I'd got over my feeling that he was spying for Mutt. Maybe he was just spying for hisself. Mutt never stood outside the window anymore. I never even saw him by accident out on the street, or down in town anywhere, and nobody I knew had seen him. I was glad. It probably meant he really was gone.

"It don't hurt anymore?" he asked.

"Naw."

He was inside me now. I was holding his back. There was still a kind of tension in my belly.

"You fine, baby," he was saying. "There's nobody like you."

I was struggling against him, trying to feel what I wasn't feeling. Then he reached down and fingered my clitoris, which made me feel more. He stopped. "Please, honey." He fingered again. I wrapped my legs around his back, the feeling inside me. Tension in my belly, like a fist drawn up. "Please." He kept on.

"What am I doing to you, Ursa? What am I doing to you?"

I kept struggling with him. I made a sound in my throat. I didn't know what he wanted me to say. What I felt didn't have words.

"Am I fucking you?"

"You fucking me."

"What are we doing, Ursa?"

"We fucking."

He dug his finger up my asshole. I contracted against him. "You fucking me. Yes, you fucking me." He fingered my clit again, but it was painful now. "It hurts," I fretted. He took his hand away. I kept moving with him, not feeling it now. I waited till his convulsions were over. His sperm inside me. Then we lay back together, exhausted, ready to sleep.

"Urs, he's going to wont more."

"He knows what I ain't got. Don't talk to me. I don't know you."

"What do you mean you don't know me? I was in your hole before he even knew you had one."

"At least I still got one, ain't I? You didn't take that away from me."

"I couldn't if I tried."

"Did you?"

Sperm to bruise me. Wash it away. Vinegar and water. Barbed wire where a womb should be. Curdled milk.

"Did I displease you so much?"

"Naw, you didn't displease me."

I came to you. Why didn't you want me? I lay on my belly waiting. That's what a woman waits for. To be fucked. A woman always waits to be fucked. Why didn't you? Now I'm without feeling.

"Was I so bad?"

"Naw, you wasn't bad."

"Did you forget so soon? I know you from way back, Ursa. That's what I said, didn't I? But you've forgotten."

"Naw I haven't forgotten. I'm still thick with you. I can't get you out."

"Does it feel good?"

"No."

"Really, Urs? Really no good?"

"Yes. I mean, I'm lying. Yes."

"What am I doing to you, Ursa?"

"You fucking me."

"I thought you were still afraid of those words."

"Didn't I tell you you taught me what Corregidora taught Great Gram. He taught her to use the kind of words she did. Don't you remember?"

"I got a terrible memory. I kept asking you, but you never would tell me . . . What am I doing?"

"You fucking me, bastard."

I dreamed that my belly was swollen and restless, and I lay without moving, gave birth without struggle, without feeling. But my eyes never turned to my feet. I never saw what squatted between my knees. But I felt the humming and beating of wings and claws in my thighs. And I felt a

stiff penis inside me. "Those who have fucked their daughters would not hesitate to fuck their own mothers." *Who are
you? Who have I born? His hair was like white wings, and
we were united at birth.*

"Who are you?"

"You don't even know your own father?"

"You not my father. I never was one of your women."

"Corregidora's women. Yes, you are."

"No!"

"What did Mutt do to you, baby?"

"I don't need your pity."

"It looks ugly in there."

"It's no worse than what you did."

"Are you sure?"

"Yes, you old bastard."

Great Gram, if she were back, what would she say?

"Be glad he didn't fuck you."

"Oh, but he did. What do you say to me now?"

"Where's the next generation?"

"Hush."

*I am Ursa Corregidora. I have tears for eyes. I was made
to touch my past at an early age. I found it on my mother's
tiddies. In her milk. Let no one pollute my music. I will dig
out their temples. I will pluck out their eyes.*

"What is it?"

"What? I'm all right."

"You weren't sleeping well again."

"I'm all right. Is it morning?"

"Almost."

"You said they never told you anything about your past.
I mean theirs. That's the same as yours."

"Naw. You know, they be some things that pass down.

But they didn't just sit me down and talk about it. But they be stories. Like, you know, about my grandmother. I took after Papa though, and the daughter that came out dark."

"Was she your mama?" I asked.

"Naw, my mama was the one that come out light."

"Aw. What else do you know?"

"Well, I know that they taught Papa how to be a blacksmith doing slavery, and when the slavery was over, he went on being a blacksmith, and then everytime he saved up some money, he'd buy a little taste of land, so the generations after him would always have land to live on. But it didn't turn out that way."

"What do you mean?"

"Well, they crooked up there. When Mama went into the courthouse to claim the land, somebody had tore one of the pages out the book. Tha's one reason I got away from up there. Aw, they let her keep the little piece of land where the house is, and I send her money every chance I get. But the rest of the land. Anyway, it's . . ."

"What?"

"Nothing. Anyway, they ain't nothing you can do when they tear the pages out of the book and they ain't no record of it. They probably burned the pages."

"*. . . Naw, I don't remember when slavery was abolished, cause I was just being born then. Mama do, and sometime it seem like I do too. They signed papers, and there wasn't all this warring like they had up here. You know, it was what they call pacific. A pacific abolition. And you know, people was celebrating and rejoicing and cheering in the street, white people and black people. And then they called Isabella, that was the princess, they started calling Isabella the Redempt'ress, you know, because she signed the paper* *with a jeweled pen. And then after that black people could go anywhere they wanted to go, and take up life anyway they wanted to take it up. And then that's when the officials burned all the papers cause they wanted to play like what had happened before never did happen. But I know it happened, I bear witness that it happened. Yeah, and Corregidora's whores was free too, but most of 'em Mama said he put down in the rut so deep, that that's bout all they could do now, though lot of 'em broke away from it too, but leastwise now they get to keep they own money and he wasn't getting hide nor hair of it. Mama stayed there with him even after it ended, until she did something that made him wont to kill her, and then she run off and had to leave me. Then he was raising me and doing you know I said what he did. But then sometime after that when she got settled here, she came back for me. That was in 1906. I was about eighteen by then. Naw, she didn't come near the place herself. She sent somebody to tell me where she was. Naw, she still think he was going to kill her. Whatever it was. By now I think he probly want to take her back, but I don't think she go back. Shortly after that I went off and met her and then we come back up to Louisiana where she was living then. Naw, I don't know what I would've done if she hadn't come. He wanted to keep me, the bastard. But it's hard to always remember what you were feeling when you ain't feeling it exactly that way no more. But when she come back for me, I was so happy I didn't know what to do, and was glad to get away from there. But by then I was big with your mama. Naw, she was born down in Louisiana. Then we come up here, you know, to get better work, and Mama was working for some Irish peoples, and I was staying home taking care of your mama and then little later on, Mama would stay at home and I was out working."*

"Didn't your daddy do anything?"

"What?"

"About the burned papers?"

"Naw, my daddy was in the war." He frowned.

"Died?"

"Naw. He went off to France during the war, and stayed in France."

I said nothing.

"You never talk about your daddy neither. It's always them women. What's your daddy like?"

"I don't know."

"What do you mean you don't know?"

"She met him when she was working down at the train depot. He just came in to get work, you know, help out and he ended up helping my mama out too, and then she had me and he went away again. He died up in New York somewhere. Some woman poisoned him. Mama never would talk about him. She said he had gypsy in him. Most of which I know my grandmama told me and told me not to tell my mama she told me. Mama never would have told me anything."

"You mixed up every which way, ain't you?"

"What do you mean?"

"You seem like you got a little bit of everything in you," he said.

"I didn't put it there," I said. I felt the resentment again, the kind I'd felt when Sal was talking to me. I didn't say anything else.

"I better get some sleep," Tadpole said. "It be 'bout time to wake up in a little while."

He turned away from me. I closed my eyes, but didn't go back to sleep. I wanted him again, but I said nothing. I waited for the alarm to go off. I stayed in bed while he got dressed to go downstairs and open up. Then I got up to get breakfast ready when he came back.

Tadpole watched me through the mirror. I was brushing my hair. We'd been married for several months now.

"Your hair's like rivers," he said.

"Is that why you married me?"

"Naw, that ain't why I married you." He laughed a little. "Naw, that's hardly why I married you."

I wanted to ask him why did he, but I was afraid to ask.

"I coulda sung with Cab Calloway," I said. "That time him and his band come out to Dixieland. He ask me to come up on stage with him, but I wouldn't do it."

"You lying."

"Naw, I ain't lying."

"Yes you are."

I grinned at him. "Yeah, I'm lying," I said. "There's a woman over on Deweese Street, though, every time she meets somebody she tells them that. I don't know if it's the truth or not. I don't even try to guess myself."

"Have you heard her sing?"

"Naw."

"Cab Calloway must've heard her do something, though?" he laughed.

I laughed, then I frowned. He saw me through the mirror. I hadn't meant for him to.

"What's wrong, Ursa?"

"Nothing."

"There's something wrong."

"Naw, they ain't."

"Come on over here, baby."

I came to him and he put his head against my belly. I had on my slip. Sometimes I went to bed in my nightgown. Sometimes I wore my slip.

"You feel all right, don't you, Ursa?"

"Yes."

"What's wrong? I know something's wrong, baby. I can tell something's been wrong."

I stroked his head, then I laughed a little. "I could've sung with Cab Calloway, that's all."

He didn't laugh.

"I love you, baby," he said.

It still got me somewhere inside when he said that, and I still couldn't bring myself to tell him the same. If he noticed it, he didn't let on. He squeezed me a little as if he were waiting for me to say something.

"If anything bothers you, Ursa, you know you can tell me. I've always been here for you to tell."

"I know, baby."

We said nothing for a long time.

"What was you doing up on that stage besides singing?" he asked, looking up at me, smiling.

"The same thing I can do here."

When we were together, he said, "I want to help you, Ursa. I want to help you as much as I can . . . Let me get up in your pussy . . . Let me get up in your pussy, baby . . . Damn, you still got a hole, ain't you? As long as a woman got a hole, she can fuck."

"I don't know if you can . . . you can't . . . I don't know if you . . ."

He was up inside me now.

"I don't want to do nothing till you ready, baby. I don't want to do it till you ready."

He was inside, and I felt nothing. I wanted to feel, but I couldn't.

"Is it good?"

"Yes."

"Is it good, baby?"

"Yes, yes."

"I just want it to feel sweet, baby. I just want it to be sweet."

"You don't have to . . ."

"I want it to be sweet for you."

I held him around his neck till I finally slept.

It was in the morning when he asked, "Did it hurt?"

"No."

He looked over at me. He had his head on the pillow, and I was looking toward him, my head almost on his chest.

"It was something. You can't tell me it wasn't," he said.

I said nothing. I kept leaning almost on his chest.

"You hurting somewhere, baby. I know you hurting somewhere."

I wished he wouldn't say that, because I wasn't sure what it meant to him.

"I'm waiting for you to tell me," he said. He seemed hard now. Before he had seemed gentle.

My chin was almost touching his chest when I said, "Let's stand."

We stood up but I couldn't get him inside me. I wanted to say, "I'm not relaxed enough," but I didn't.

He stroked me on the behind, pulling up on me, then he said, "You have to work too." He pulled up on me more, squatting down. He took me with him to the wall, squatting more. I still couldn't get him in.

"Work, Ursa."

"I *am* working," I said. It was almost a cry, but a cry I didn't want him to hear. I don't know how long it was between it and when I finally said, "Tadpole, I can't, I can't."

He stood watching me for a moment, and then he said, "Well, I'm not going to stand here all day."

He walked away from me and went in the bathroom.

I stood facing the wall, remembering that time I wanted it but Mutt was angry and wouldn't give it to me.

"Don't bring it here," he had said.

I bent down then to kiss him.

"I said, 'Don't bring it here, Urs.'"

"I just want to kiss you."

He turned away. "Shit, I know how it is. Mens just hanging in there trying to get some. It's the Happy Café awright. Mens just hanging around so they can get something."

"Mutt, you know it ain't that kind of a place. Tadpole don't run that kind of a place."

"I bet if I went over to one a those tables and I asked them what they have and they would tell me the truth about it, they'd say, 'Piece a tail, please,' and I asked them 'What tail' they say, 'That woman's standing up there. That good-lookin woman standin right up there.' Shit, I know how mens is. They just be laying in your ass if they could."

"You know I ain't give it to nobody else."

"How I know?" He turned on me, his eyes narrowed, then he turned his back to me. I tried to turn him back around, but gave up trying.

"Mutt, please," I said quietly.

"I said, 'Don't bring it here.'"

That was all he said. He made sounds like he was sleeping. I thought he was, until he asked me, quieter than I'd heard him ask anything, "Tell me if they ain't asked you."

I tried to touch him again.

"I said I don't want it," he said.

That time I'd gone in the bathroom.

When Tad came back, I was still facing the wall. I could feel him near me, but I didn't turn around.

"I knew about that other shit in the hospital," he said coldly.

"What shit?" I turned around.

"I mean that *other* shit," he said.

I was afraid to ask more. I knew by his look what he meant, and I was afraid that if I moved too far, he'd move farther. I held my stomach and turned back around to the wall. He walked on behind me and went downstairs to work.

One evening after I'd finished singing, a man came up to me and offered me a job singing Saturday nights at the Spider. I talked to Tadpole about it.

"Do whatever you want to," he said. "You your own woman."

I couldn't tell whether he wanted me to take it, or he was thinking too much about what caused the trouble between Mutt and me. I wanted to take it, because I wanted the change. It was different living there now, *and* working there. I felt different.

"I'd like to take it," I said. "You could probably get Eddy's combo to come back on Saturdays, don't you think?"

"You your own woman," he repeated.

I didn't say anything else. I telephoned the man and said I'd take the job. I had a two-hour show on Saturdays, playing piano and singing. Tadpole had Joe Williams playing piano for me there. Tadpole would come to pick me up after work. He came to pick me up the first night.

"Did you get Eddy's?"

"Naw, I got a girl," he said.

"Oh. Is she any good?"

"I think so."

Her show had ended when I got back, so I didn't see her, but Sal said she couldn't've been more than fifteen.

Once when I was playing piano at the Spider, Jim came in. He was as surprised to see me as I was to see him. In fact, he looked like he couldn't believe I was there. And I hadn't reckoned with what his being there meant. If Jim could come in, I was thinking . . . I went on singing. There was a break between hours, and when I finished, Jim came up to say something to me.

"What is it?" I asked. I was sitting on the piano stool. He was standing with his drink.

"You stop working for your old man?" he asked.

"I still work there," I said.

"But you work here too?"

"Yeah."

"He got a pretty little thing working over there. I was over there last Saturday. I didn't ask about you. I just assumed you wasn't working." He looked at me. I knew what he was thinking.

"Naw, I'm working," I said.

"You get paid more over here?" he asked.

"Yes, but that's not my reason."

"You just wanted a little change of pace, that's all?"

"I guess so. Look, I better get back to work. That's what he pays me for."

He nodded, and went back and sat at his table. I could've taken a longer break but I just didn't want to talk to him. He left shortly afterwards. I didn't see him the next Saturday, but I finally saw the girl. She came in once during the supper show and went over and said something to Tadpole. She had long straightened hair and eyeliner around her eyes. She looked fifteen and older than fifteen. After she finished talking to Tadpole she went out. When I finished singing, I asked Sal if that was the one. "Yeah," she said. "Her name's Vivian. Fast little nigger." I didn't say anything to Tadpole about her. I kept going my Saturdays to the Spider, and Tadpole would come and pick me up afterwards.

But one night he didn't come and pick me up, and I took a cab home. When I got there Sal was still there, and Thedo was behind the bar.

"What's wrong?" I asked. "Where's Tad?"

"He had to go out somewhere," she said. She acted nervous. "Come over and have a drink with me."

"Where'd he go?"

"He didn't say where he was going. Come over and have a drink."

"He could've called me," I said. I went over to the bar with her, but then I turned and said I was going upstairs.

"She's up there with him," Thedo said in his low voice.

"Thedo," Sal said.

I went upstairs. I knew what I'd find. Tadpole drunk and that hussy in bed with him. I opened the door.

Tadpole looked up. They weren't doing anything now, but they'd been doing it. I came in the room.

"Get your ass out of my bed," I told the girl. She wasn't drunk or afraid of me, but she got up and started dressing. She seemed to be making fun of me without saying it, or even smiling. "If you want something to fuck, I'll give you my fist to fuck," I said, surprised at the words I'd echoed. I didn't touch her though. I just stood there watching her. She dressed as she would have dressed if I hadn't even been in there.

"Now, honey, you don't have to go on like that," Tadpole said. He was still in bed. "And Vive, honey, you don't have to leave."

Vivian dressed, told Tadpole she'd see him and went past me out the door.

"You see me," I said, but she'd already left. She hadn't closed the door. I closed the door.

"What right you got coming in here?" he asked.

"I'm your wife," I said.

"What do you do?" he asked.

I said nothing. I just looked at him. He was raising up, but then lay back down.

"Come on over here, baby."

I didn't move.

"You goddamn bastard," I said.

"You ain't got no right to go on like that," he said. "We wasn't doing nothing. I wasn't doing nothing but sucking on her tiddies."

"I don't give a damn what you was sucking on. Or what she was sucking on either."

"Do more for me than yours does."

"Shut up."

"Her tiddies do more for me than your goddamn pussy-hole do."

"Shut up, nigger."

"Nigger, yourself. You can't even *come* with me. You don't even know what to do with a *real* man. I bet you couldn't even come with him when you *had* something up in there. Don't give me that shit about he didn't wont you to work no more. A man wants a woman that can do something for him."

"You know what you can do for me."

"I know what you *can't* do."

"You knew what happened to me when you married me," I said.

"I know some women that can fuck your ass off you too after it happened to *them*."

"How do you know you a real man?" I said. "If you had to leave me for somebody that ain't even a real woman yet."

"She got more woman in her asshole than you got in your whole goddamn cunt."

I said nothing. I was holding back too much now. Then I said, "If you wanted to get rid of me, you didn't have to do it this way. It's not me, it's *you*."

I went out, leaving the door open. When I got downstairs I said nothing to either Sal or Thedo. I walked out. There was no Cat's to go to now. I checked in at the Drake Hotel. I'd kept from crying until I got in the room, and then I couldn't keep from crying.

Because I knew why he kept me waiting, Cat, that's why I knew what you felt, why I wouldn't tell you that I knew. A man always says I want to fuck, a woman always has to say I want to get fucked. Does it feel good? And all those dreams I had lying there in the hospital about being screwed and not feeling anything. Numb between my legs. Part of it was what I needed to make myself feel, what I had to know. Okay, I'll admit that now. But what changes? Mutt doesn't change. I couldn't go back to Tadpole, either. Not that he'd take me back, getting what he wants. What I feel crawling under my skin. That fifteen-year-old heifer. Even I didn't have eyes like that. What she needs is some of Cat's medicine. That would tame her. What am I thinking? Afraid only of what I'll become, because those times he didn't touch the clit, I couldn't feel anything, and then he . . . Why won't you, honey? But he turned away. Anyway, you knew what was wrong before you snatched after my ass. No, what's inside my head because those other women they could do it. Afraid of what I. No, I didn't push it, Cat. He wanted it too. He pushed it too. But with a man,

*it's easy to just push it away. The doctor said there wasn't
anything wrong with me, Cat. I didn't go back, because
there was nothing wrong, and he said it looked all right
down there. I felt all right, and my strength is back. Why
won't you turn back toward me? I'm so tired of waiting.
Afraid of waiting. I gave you what I could. You didn't ask
for that. You knew about the scar on my belly. You didn't
ask for children that I couldn't give. What I wanted too.
Afraid of what I'll come to. All that sweat in my hands.
What can you do for me?*

    "What bothers you?"
    "It bothers me because I can't make generations."
    "What bothers you?"
    "It bothers me because I can't."
    "What bothers you, Ursa?"
    "It bothers me because I can't fuck."
    "What bothers you, Ursa?"
    "It bothers me because I can't feel anything."
    "I told you that nigger couldn't do nothing for you."
    "You liar. You didn't tell me nothing. You left me when
you threw me down those . . ."

It was a couple of days after I'd found them together,
that there was a knock on the door. I hadn't left the room
in those two days, mostly lay on the bed, sent down for
some coffee. When I opened the door it was Tadpole. I
didn't shut it. I didn't ask him to come in. I stood aside,
and he came in. He stood there, looking at me. I still had
on the dress I'd sung in, and I must've looked bad.

    "This ain't good for you," he said.

    I didn't answer him. I shut the door, though.

    "I gave myself hell," he said. "That was the first time,
Urs."

"First time is always a beginning," I said, still standing near the door. "It's what you wanted."

"Urs."

"Naw, Tad, cause when you got that girl there you was thinking it."

"We've got to work something out, Urs."

"Work what out? Little piece on the side? You be having me, but you gonna be having her, ain't you? When? Every time I go to the Spider, she be performing up in my bed."

"I was drunk, Ursa."

"I was sober, and I got a good memory."

"I gave myself hell."

"She still working for you, though, ain't she?"

"Yeah, she need the job, baby. She . . . she not well taken care of."

I laughed.

"Urs, you know you the only woman I want. I love you, Urs."

"What about your other need?" I looked at him hard. "Naw, Tad."

He'd started getting close to me, and put himself up against me, squeezing my ass.

"Baby."

"Tadpole, go away, please!"

"That was the first time, Ursa!"

"Won't be the last, will it?"

He just looked at me. I turned away from him. There was silence for a long time. I could feel him behind me. Then: "What are you going to do, fuck yourself?" he asked.

The door slammed.

I stayed in that room for two more days, and then I went to talk about getting on full time at the Spider.

I got on full time, and I guess Vivian was on full time with Tadpole. The Spider was way on the other side of town, and I hoped I wouldn't have to run into either of them. I did see Vivian once, though, but played like I didn't know who she was. We were standing on different sides of the street. She was waiting on the bus going out East End and I was waiting on the one going out West. She kept looking at me, though, as if she expected me or wanted me to come over and say something to her, but I just gave her that "I'm not studying you, Vivian" look. She looked really run-down and bad too, or maybe I was just imagining she did. But I'm sure anybody who didn't know her would've thought she was a woman in her twenties instead of fifteen or sixteen or however old she was now.

"That's that woman that sing out to Happy's Café, ain't it?"

"What?"

"That's that woman that sing out to Happy's, ain't it?" the woman beside me asked.

"Yeah, I think so," I said.

"You got a hard kind of voice," Max said one day. Max Monroe was the man that owned the place. He didn't try to make me, because he knew how I felt about it. He had once, though, but I'd set him straight. I was in the back room having coffee when he came in. It was between shows. Sometimes Max would be there for both shows. Sometimes he would be there just for the last show, and then close up. He was a square-shouldered man in his early fifties. When he came in, he was laughing.

"What is it?" I asked.

He went over and got himself some coffee.

"Naw, it's just these people that live up top of me," he

was saying. "Get drunk and argue and then in the morning forget what they were arguing about. Still mad, but don't even know what it was for."

I said nothing. He sat down in one of the chairs, the one nearest me.

"Yeah, if you ever live in a rooming house, you got some crazy people, always keep you laughing."

"I bet," I said.

I didn't like him so close, and I didn't really know how to be friendly with him. When he talked to you, he liked to get right up in your face. I'd observed him with other people and he'd get up close to them too. Like if he was in a chair talking to somebody, he'd pull his chair up closer. He'd never made a pass at me or anything like that, but I still felt awkward. I remember once I was sitting outside just before opening, and he'd come over and talked to me, and instead of sitting in one of the chairs, he'd squatted down next to my lap and started talking. I'd wanted to move away, but I knew I couldn't, and there was nothing in his eyes to make me feel it was for any bad reason. Now he pulled his chair up close to mine.

"How was the first show?"

"It went pretty well."

"Lot of people out here tonight. We been doing good business since you been here."

"Thank you."

"Real good business. I knew when I seen you, get you here and we'd be doing good business. Something powerful about you."

I said nothing.

"Something real powerful."

I kept wondering if he were sober or drunk. I kept looking at him, and he kept looking sober.

"Yeah, that man and that woman's crazy." He was laughing again. "Just arguing up there all night long, and then in the morning don't even know what they arguing about."

"People's like that," I said.

"Yeah, they is, ain't they?" He was shaking his head. "I ain't never married myself. Cause I seen too many crazy womens . . . I don't mean nothing by you."

I laughed.

"I'm only kidding. It just ain't struck my fancy. Or I guess no woman ain't struck my fancy. I been a loner most of my life. Grew up as one and grew old as one."

"You not old."

He said nothing. He drank some more coffee and put his cup down. He reached over and touched me on the shoulder. I tried not to move. Sometimes I found myself not knowing how much men did meant friendly and how much meant something else. Or maybe I was just kidding myself. I wouldn't let myself tell whether it was a fatherly touch, or whether I should take my hand and remove his.

"You know you really helped this place. I ain't never heard nobody sang like you, and guess I never will. Naw, it wasn't nothing before you come. I hope you know this. I always feel awkward saying stuff like this, Ursa, but I just wont you to know how much I appreciate you being here. How much you doing for this place."

I said, "Thank you."

I kept waiting for him to remove his hand, but he didn't. When he tried to reach down between my breasts, I jumped up and almost spilled the coffee on him. It fell on the floor, some splattering against the hem of my dress.

"Naw," I kept saying, "naw."

"I didn't mean you no harm, baby. You know I wouldn't do nothing to hurt you. I didn't mean you no harm, honey."

He kept trying to pat me up but I kept moving away from him, till I got against the wall.

"Don't come over here no further, Max," I said.

He didn't. I kept looking at him. I knew he was sober.

"It ain't that way, Max. It ain't gon be that way."

"I didn't mean you no harm." He reached out his hand, but my look must have stopped him. He straightened his shoulders. "I really don't," he insisted.

"That looked like harm to me," I said quietly.

"It wasn't."

I tried to laugh. "A helping hand, I suppose?"

"If you want it to be that."

"I don't want it to be anything." I kept my eyes hard. "Always been that way, ain't it?"

"What way?"

"What you can get. Think you can get something. I mean some. When I was a little girl I used to go over with my mama to the beauty parlor. There was this man that just hang around there all the time. Mama asked me to wait outside for her, 'cause she wasn't going in there but for a minute. He come around me. You know, I was a friendly little girl then, I didn't know no better. He come over by me holding his hand out. 'Gimme what you got. What you gonna gimme? Gimme what you got.' He kept laughing. When Mama come out, she looked at that man real evil, and grabbed my hand and pulled me on away from there. When she got me home, she said didn't I see what that man was doing, he was reaching for me down between my legs. I just thought he was holding his hand out."

He looked hurt. "I ain't that man. I ain't like that. I didn't mean you no harm. You know a man gets . . ." He didn't finish.

"I know too well how a man gets," I said.

"I wasn't trying to make you or nothing like that. I just..."

"Don't lie, Max. I don't wont no lying," I said, and then I was thinking perhaps he *wasn't* lying, perhaps he didn't want to make me, just wanted to be hugged and touched. I said nothing else.

"You mad at me?"

He had straightened up even more now. Somehow I'd never really pictured him as being after women. If he had a woman, I'd never seen him with her, and I'd never been in the habit of asking around about people.

I didn't answer his question.

"You gon still work for me?" he asked.

"If we keep things the way they was. Otherwise, I'ma walk out. I don't know where I'm walking to, but I'ma go somewhere."

He stood there saying nothing. I almost thought he would let me leave.

"You know you too good to lose," he said finally.

"You won't touch me no more?" It was more of a plea than a question.

"Honey, I ain't gonna lay a hand on you."

"I'ma go home and change," I said.

He stood aside and let me pass.

Before I got to the door, he said, "I know how you feel about it now. There won't be no more."

I turned around and looked at him and smiled a little, then I went out the door.

"You got a hard kind of voice," he said now. "You know, like callused hands. Strong and hard but gentle underneath. Strong but gentle too. The kind of voice that can hurt you. I can't explain it. Hurt you and make you still want to listen."

"If you can't explain it, I can't explain it," I said, thinking about what Cat had said what seemed like a long time ago now. "But I think I know what you mean," I added.

He smiled. He was only friendly now. Nothing romantic. He knew I'd meant what I said.

"You a hard woman to get into," he said. Then he looked embarrassed, because he hadn't meant it the way I could have taken it to mean.

"You wouldn't want to try, would you?" I said.

"I guess not," he said, and got up.

I wouldn't have known what else to say if he'd stayed. I went back to the piano.

"*Ursa, have you lost the blues?*"
"*Naw, the blues is something you can't loose.*"
"*Gimme a feel. Just a little feel.*"
"*You had your feel.*"
"*Are you lonely?*"
"*Yes.*"
"*Do you still fight the night?*"
"*Yes.*"
"*Lonely blues. Don't you care if you see me again?*"
"*Naw, I don't care.*"
"*Don't you want your original man?*"
"*Naw, I . . .*"
"*I know what he did to your voice.*"
"*What you did.*"
"*Still, they can't take it away from you. But ain't nothing better for the blues than a good . . .*"
"*Don't, Mutt.*"
"*Come over here, honey.*"
"*Naw.*"
"*I need somebody.*"
"*Naw.*"

"*I said I need somebody.*"

"*Naw.*"

"*I won't treat you bad.*"

"*Naw.*"

"*I won't make you sad.*"

"*Naw.*"

"*Come over here, honey, and visit with me a little.*"

"*Naw.*"

"*Come over here, baby, and visit with me a little.*"

"*Naw.*"

"*You got to come back to your original man.*"

"*Naw. What you did.*"

"*Just give me a little feel. You lonely, ain't you?*"

"*I been there awready.*"

"*Then you know what I need. Put me in the alley, Urs.*"

"*Something wrong with me down there.*"

"*I still wont to get in your alley, baby.*"

"*Naw, Mutt.*"

"*What you looking for, anyway, woman?*"

"*What we stopped being to each other.*"

"*I never knew what we was.*"

"*Something you gave me once, but stopped giving me.*"

"*I want to fuck you.*"

"*That ain't what I mean.*"

"*I still want to fuck you.*"

"*What you stopped giving me.*"

"*I still want to fuck you.*"

"*Naw.*"

"*What he stopped giving you too?*"

"*Yes.*"

"*What you need?*"

"*Yes.*"

"*What you wanted from me?*"

"Yes."

"What you wanted from anybody?"

"Naw."

"I still want to fuck you."

"Yes, fuck me."

"Let me get behind you."

"Naw."

"Sit on my lap then."

"Naw, I don't want it that way."

"Then fuck you."

"So that's how the ole man made all his money."

"Yeah, that's how he made it."

"Forget what they went through."

"I can't forget."

"Forget what you been through."

"I can't forget. The space between my thighs. A well that never bleeds."

"And who are you fucking?"

"No one. Silence in my womb. My breasts quiver like old apples."

"Forget the past."

"I can't. Somebody called me over the telephone and said he was making a survey. He didn't sound right to me, but I asked him what he wanted anyway. He said, 'How do it feel?' I just hung up."

"That's too much mascara you're using, and those shadows."

"I made them, to cover up the ones that are really there."

"Tell me, Ursa, do insanity run in your family?"

"Corregidora, he went mad."

"They all do."

"Ursa, I want you again."

"We give each other too much hell."

"I never stopped loving you."

"Hush."

"Do it for me. I haven't forgotten."

"I have."

"Forget the past, except ours, the good feeling."

"What about . . ."

"That was an accident. If I could, I'd give it back to you, but I can't. I'll let you take me inside you."

"It's good to feel your breath near me."

"Your original man."

"They told me what happened to you, baby."

"Who's they?"

"Yeah, they told me what happened. But you ain't got nothing to worry about, though. You still got a hole, ain't you? Long as a woman got a hole, she can fuck. Let me get up in your hole, baby."

"Leave me alone."

"Let me get up in your hole, I said. I wont to get up in your goddamn hole."

"I wanted to give you something, Mutt, but now I can't give you anything. I never told you how it was. Always their memories, but never my own. They slept in the bedroom and I slept on a trundle bed in the front room. An old slop jar behind their bed. I can remember how big the bed looked when I was sitting on the slop jar. Big enough to hide behind. The two women in that house. The three of them at first and then when I was older, just the two of them, one sitting in a rocker, the other in a straight-back chair, telling me things. I'd always listen. I never saw my mama with a man, never ever saw her with a man. But she *wasn't a virgin because of me. And still she was heavy with virginity. Her swollen belly with no child inside. And still she never had a man. Or never let me see her with one. No, I think she never had one. They kept to the house, telling me things. My mother would work while my grandmother told me, then she'd come home and tell me. I'd go to school and come back and be told. When I was real little, Great Gram rocking me and talking. And still it was as if my mother's whole body shook with that first birth and memories and she wouldn't make others and she wouldn't give those to me, though she passed the other ones down, the monstrous ones, but she wouldn't give me her own terrible ones. Loneliness. I could feel it, like she was breathing it, like it was all in the air. Desire, too. I couldn't recognize it then. But now when I look back, that's all I see. Desire, and loneliness. A man that left her. Still she carried their evidence, screaming, fury in her eyes, but she wouldn't give me that, not that one. Not her private memory. And then when Grandmama told me I hid my face in the pillow and cried. I couldn't tell her I knew. I could see her strong eyes full of fury, what she'd kept so long. And I kept waiting for her to tell me, but she wouldn't tell me. Sometimes I'd try to feel it out of her with my eyes, but I couldn't get it. No. She was closed up like a fist. It was her very own memory, not theirs, her very own real and terrible and lonely and dark memory. And I never saw her with a man because she wouldn't give them anything else. Nothing. And still she told me what I should do, that I should make generations. But it was almost as if she'd left him too, as if she wanted only the memory to keep for her own but not his fussy body, not the man himself. Almost as if she'd gone out to get that man to have me and then didn't need him, because they'd been telling her so often what she should do. But he left before she could leave.*

Wasn't it that? Wasn't it you gave me something that I couldn't give back? And her body shook with the fury of my birth. She said I came into the world complaining, they didn't have to slap me. Into the world, her incomplete world, full of teeth and memories, repeating never her own to me. Never her own. And I remember now, I didn't feel it then, I never saw her with a man, never saw her with a man. I didn't feel it then, because they were all my world. And I never saw her with a man . . .

Something she kept not to be given. As if she'd already given. There was things left, yes. It wasn't the kind of giving where there's nothing left. It's where what's left is something you keep with you, something you don't give. I mean, the first giving made what's left. Created it. Do you understand? You nod your head, but do you really? And we'd have steaming cups of cocoa and remember. Corregidora, who gave orders to whores, the father of his daughter and his daughter's daughter. "How can it be?" Mama would ask. And when she talked, Mutt, it was like she had something else behind her eyes. Corregidora was easier than what she wouldn't tell me. They'd look at her. They'd tell theirs and then they'd look at her to bear them witness. But what could she say? She could only tell me what they'd told her. How can it be? She was the only one who asked that question, though. For the others it was just something that was, something they had, and something they told. But when she talked, it was like she was asking that question for them, and for herself too. Sometimes I wonder about their desire, you know. Grandmama's and Great Gram's. Corregidora was theirs more than hers. Mama could only know, but they could feel. They were with him. What did they feel? You know how they talk about hate and desire. Two humps on the same camel? Yes. Hate and desire both riding them, that's what I was going to say. "You carry more than his name, Ursa," Mama would tell me. And I knew she had more than their memories. Something behind her eyes. A knowing, a feeling of her own. But she'd speak only their life. What was their life then? Only a life spoken to the sounds of my breathing or a low-playing Victrola. Mama's Christian songs, and Grandmama—wasn't it funny—it was Grandmama who liked the blues. But still Mama would say listening to the blues and singing them ain't the same. That's what she said when I asked her how come she didn't mind Grandmama's old blues records. What's a life always spoken, and only spoken? Still there was what they never spoke, Mutt, what even they wouldn't tell me. How all but one of them had the same lover? Did they begrudge her that? Was that their resentment? There was something, Mutt. They squeezed Corregidora into me, and I sung back in return. I would have rather sung her memory if I'd had to sing any. What about my own? Don't ask me that now. But do you think she knew? Do you think that's why she kept it from me? Oh, I don't mean in the words, I wouldn't have done that. I mean in the tune, in the whole way I drew out a song. In the way my breath moved, in my whole voice. How could she bear witness to what she'd never lived, and refuse me what she had lived? That's what I mean.

But look at me, though, I am not Corregidora's daughter. Look at me, I am not Corregidora's daughter."

"Stop, Ursa, why do you go on making dreams?"

"Till I feel satisfied that I could have loved, that I could have loved you, till I feel satisfied, alone, and satisfied that I could have loved."

"Do you still hate me?"

"Yes. In the hospital, standing over me. You. I hated you. I cussed you. And I've got more hurt now than then. How do you think I feel? Why did you come back, anyway?"

"I came to get you."

"He made them make love to anyone, so they couldn't love anyone."

"You'll come back."

"If I do, I'll come with all my memories. I won't forget anything."

"I'd rather have you with them, than not have you."

"Mutt, don't."

I couldn't be satisfied until I had seen Mama, talked to her, until I had discovered her private memory. One Saturday morning I went down to the bus station.

I hadn't expected Bracktown to change, and it hadn't. When I stepped off the bus, there was Mr. Deak's store right where it had always been, with the tall porch, and those concrete steps leading up to it, except the steps used to be wooden and rickety, so I guess the concrete was a change. And it looked like he had painted the door. I didn't go in to say anything to him, because I knew he'd get to talking and asking me how things was, and telling me about everybody I didn't want to hear about. I hoped he hadn't seen me from the door, though, because then he mighta thought I'd got too uppity to stop in and say something to him. I went across the railroad track and started down the dirt road. I don't know how long they'd been talking about paving it, and still hadn't. It was all right when it wasn't raining, but when it rained there wasn't nothing out there but mud. A group of people were going to go into Versailles and have them come out and tar the road, but I don't know what came of that. Maybe the people in Versailles said that Bracktown wasn't a part of Versailles, even though they had their post office there, and went to school in Versailles. Bracktown was one of those little towns set back from the highway. All you could see

from the highway was Mr. Deak's store, and if you weren't
from the area, you wouldn't even know Bracktown was
there. It wasn't really big enough to be called a town, anyway. About twenty or thirty families lived there and so
they called it a town. All it had there really was Mr. Deak's
store, which did more business from the highway than from
the town, though that was the only place the town people
had to go, and there was a restaurant that was more somebody's house than a restaurant, and a church that must've
been one of the smallest churches in the country. The town
had a woman like Cat who straightened hair or, rather,
who straightened hair like Cat, except she was considered
the authorized beautician and had set up a beauty parlor
in the basement of her house, and instead of a barber shop,
there was a man who cut hair in his front room or sometimes
while they were congregated down at Mr. Deak's store.
Just a pair of scissors and a comb and his haircuts looked
better than the ones in the city. His name was Mr. Grundy.
I thought he would change, but he didn't. The last time I
was here, when Grandmama died, he still had that pair of
scissors and the comb. The older men still kept him, but the
younger ones, who had started wearing afros, were saying
they had their own scissors and comb. Mr. Grundy said,
then they never used the scissors and he wasn't too sure
they used the comb. In the summertime, he would sit his
barber's chair, which was really a kitchen chair, out on the
side of the road. I passed some women coming down the
road, probably on their way up to Deak's. I spoke but they
looked at me kind of evil. All I could think of was those
women in church that time, when I first came back, telling
Mama I must be some new woman in town who be trying
to take their husbands. I laughed, then I frowned. I couldn't
even take my own husband, I was thinking. When I had
come back for Grandmama's funeral, though, there had

been this one old woman, who had kept looking at me. She had just kept looking at me. She'd looked at me when we were in the church, and then when we were out at the cemetery, she'd stood next to me. I kept feeling she was going to say something to me, but she didn't until the burial was over and we were going back. She didn't walk well, and was carrying a cane.

"Ain't you Ursa?"

I said, "Yes."

"I thought you was. You look just like your grandmama did when she was your age. You don't look like your mama, you look more like your grandmama. Last time I seen you you wasn't big as my stick. Now you a woman."

I had smiled at her, but didn't know what to say.

"I know you don't remember me, honey. You don't have to say nothing."

I had felt bad, but then a man had come and taken her arm. Then I recognized her because I recognized the man. The man was Mr. Floyd. And she was Mr. Floyd's mother.

Mr. Floyd was the man who lived across the road from our house, in a trailer. Everybody had a house out there, except him, but the trailer had stayed put like a house. It must have been before or during the time I was born that he first come out there, because I always remembered seeing him. He was about Mama's age. Sometimes I would wonder how much he knew, but I'd never had the nerve to ask him. Ever since I was growing up he'd never come over to visit us and we'd never gone to visit him. Mama said he wasn't nothing but a hermit. But she didn't dislike him the way Grandmama used to act like she did. I'd only remembered seeing Mr. Floyd's mother once or twice, and she'd only spoken to Grandmama when we'd all happened to be in Mr. Deak's store at the same time. She'd asked my grandmother if she'd ever been to Midway, and my grandmother had told her no.

"You look like a woman that . . ."

My grandmother had looked at her hard, and then Mr. Floyd's mother had looked at me, and said nothing else.

Grandmama waited for Mr. Floyd and his mama to leave, and then we left.

I smiled now because I saw that chair sitting out on the side of the road. Mr. Grundy and three men, one sitting and the other two standing, either waiting for their turns, or just talking. Probably seen Mr. Grundy out there with this other man, and just stopped out there talking. They said, "How do?" I said, "How do?" back to them, and you know how men's eyes widen when some new and halfway-decent-looking woman passes. Sometimes she don't even have to be halfway-decent-looking, just new. I wondered what would have happened if I'd seen the women and the men at the same time, and the women had seen how the men were looking. They would've thought for sure I was after somebody's husband then.

"You Miss Corregidora's girl?" This was Grundy.

"Yes." I stopped.

"Well I be. You sho have growed. You was out here couple of years ago, though, wasn't you, when the old lady passed. I was scared to say anything to you then, scared you wouldn't know me. But seem like you changed again."

"Heavier."

"I wish my lady was heavy like that," said the man seated.

"Too young for you, Mose," said one of the other men.

"Mose think he still thirty," said the other man, laughing.

"Well, I know your mama gon be glad to see you, honey," Mr. Grundy said, trying to quiet the other men.

I smiled and went on down the road.

"Man, you spose to be cuttin my *hair*."

"Have some respect."

After I'd got on full time at the Spider, I'd asked Mama if she wanted to come live with me in the city, but she'd said Naw, said she felt peaceful where she was. I wasn't sure what she meant by "peaceful," but I thought, peaceful or not, she wouldn't have left that house. Too many memories. And I was almost beginning to be sure, more her own, than *theirs*. The lived life, not the spoken one. When I came up to the house it was the same one, the little wooden porch that looked too small for the swing that was on it, the honeysuckle bush, an old wicker rocker. And Mr. Floyd's trailer was still there, across the road, and a truck patch he must've just started. I knocked on the front, but Mama didn't hear me, so I walked around to the back. I left some avocados I'd brought her on the porch, telling myself it was so they'd get ripe, but the real reason I was thinking was Mama might feel I thought I couldn't come unless I brought something, but that was silly. I knocked on the back door. She heard me.

"Ursa," she said. "Hi you, honey."

"Hi, Mama." I went over and kissed her.

She was standing up at the stove, stirring some preserves. She canned things for people. They would provide the strawberries or whatever it was, and she would can them. The other thing she did, which I didn't like, especially now that I could send her more money, was work three days out of each week for some white woman who lived in Midway, who'd come and get her and drive her back. I kept hoping she would stop, but so far she hadn't.

"Whose preserves?" I asked.

"Mr. Floyd's," she said. "His or his mama's. I think he's gon give em to her."

She had gotten bigger around the waist, and looked like Grandmama and Great Gram used to look, the graying hair plaited on the sides and tied in a knot in the back, the way she had been beginning to look just before I left, the way I knew I would look when I got her age. I was in my late thirties and she was in her late fifties. She had stopped stirring to hug me. Now she turned the fire down.

"I missed you," she said.

I told her I missed her too. I always felt awkward saying things like that. I went over and sat down at the kitchen table. I was wondering if she would have said I missed you if she knew why I'd come. She stood with her back to me for a moment, and then she turned the fire off completely, put the cover on the pot, and came and sat down at the table opposite me.

"Do you want something? I've got some ham in there and I could scramble you up some eggs."

"No, I'm all right," I said.

"You sure?"

I said, "Yes."

She sat with her hands on the table.

"It's good to see you, baby," she said again.

I looked away. It was almost like I was realizing for the first time how lonely it must be for her with them gone, and that maybe she was even making a plea for me to come back and be a part of what wasn't any more.

"You look like a gypsy, them beads on."

I told her they were trade beads, what they used to use for money over in Europe somewhere. I didn't know where in Europe. She only nodded.

"You here for a long visit or a short one?" she asked finally.

"Naw, I didn't bring anything, Mama. I'm not staying. I'm getting back on the bus at three-thirty."

She looked away from me this time.

"I brought you some avocados," I said. "I left them out on the porch."

"They so expensive, Ursa. I was down to the store, and Mr. Deak was selling them for fifty cents a piece."

"I know how you like them."

She said, "Thank you." She looked away from me again. I could feel the strain and wondered if she could. I'd always loved her and knew she loved me, but still somehow we'd never "talked" things before, and I wanted to talk things now.

I put my hands up on the table. "Mama."

"What is it?" She looked at me quickly.

"Grandmama told me something."

She looked away. She was still beautiful, in *their* way of still being beautiful, and the way I knew I would still be beautiful when I got to be their age. I could see her mouth tighten. Her own hands had left the table and gone into her lap. She still had her apron on.

"She told me about the man you met at the train depot where you used to work. She told me how you met my father."

"What you want, Ursa?" she asked quietly.

"Nothing you don't want to give, but I hope you'll want to give it."

She was silent, then she said, "Suppose I told you I don't want to give it, I never wanted to give it."

"I'd ask you what you meant."

She laughed a little, the kind of laugh that's not really a laugh, as if one had to make more effort to get a laugh, and she hadn't made enough effort.

"It's not that I don't want to talk to my baby," she said. "I want to talk to you, Ursa."

"But you can't."

"No."

"You could try."

She said nothing. She still hadn't looked at me.

"*They* knew. If I came back to live with you, I'd have to know too." I hadn't intended to say that, and didn't like why I might have said it. I added quickly, "But I can't come back and live with you. I have to make my own kind of life. I have to make some kind of life for myself."

"I knew how situations was with you and Tadpole," she said.

I didn't ask her how she knew. There was always someone running to tell things like that. I looked away from her for a moment and then when I looked back at her she was looking at me. It was a quiet look. It was as if she were waiting for me to make her talk. I just kept looking at her, hoping that what was in my look would make her.

"Corregidora's never been enough for you, has it?" she asked.

"No."

"I thought it would be."

"What happened with you was always more important. What happened with you and him."

Her face tightened for a moment.

"Corregidora is responsible for that part of my life. If Corregidora hadn't happened that part of my life never would have happened."

"Wouldn't it?" My eyes narrowed a little, but not in a way, I hoped, that would make her stop.

She didn't answer. I wanted to ask her if *their* past could really have had so much to do with her own, but I just kept watching her. I wanted my eyes to say it. Some things I had to let my eyes say.

"He wasn't a man I met at no depot." She was shaking her head, looking away from me again. "Naw, I didn't meet him at no depot. He worked at this place across the road from the depot, where I used to go in to have lunch. I didn't pay him no mind. He used to stand behind that counter watching me, and I never did pay him no mind. He was a good-lookin man, I guess. Yeah, your daddy was a good-lookin man. Tall and straight as a arrow. Black man. You know, kind of satin-black. Smooth satin-black. You come out lookin more like me than you did like him, I mean about the color. You got long legs like he had. Sometimes during his breaks he'd sit down at one of the tables, and cross his legs twice. You know how some people can do, cross their legs and then bring his foot around, you know, like he was winding his legs around each other. I used to try to do it. I never could though. I bet you can. I wasn't studyin him, though, cause you know then I wasn't lookin for a man. They'd tell me, they'd be telling me about making generations, but I wasn't out looking for no man. I never was out looking for no man. I kept thinking back on it, though, and it was like I had to go there, had to go there and sit there and have him watch me like that. Sometimes he'd be cleaning the counter and watching me, you know how mens watch you when they wont something. It don't have to be to open your legs up, though most times it is. Sometimes I think he wonted something else, and then sometimes I think that's all he wonted. I wasn't out looking for him, I know that, and he never did say nothing to me neither, except this one time. See, I'd always been coming to lunch, and then this one time I come in there and had supper too. Mama and your Great Gram was having something at church, and said they wouldn't be home for dinner, and I didn't wont to sit up in the house and eat by myself, so I went over there. I was going to go over there, you know, and then come on home, maybe listen to the radio or read something, and then go on to bed. I went over there and ate my supper. He looked like he was surprised to see me when I come in. But this time instead of just taking my plate away, he stopped there and said something to me. He said it real soft. It was almost like I didn't hear him, but I knew I heard him. I wasn't even looking at him. I wouldn't even look up from the table. He was standing there looking down at me. He said 'Hello' real soft. I wouldn't even look up at him though. I talked back to him, soft too, but I wouldn't look up at him.

" 'Hello.'

" 'Hello.'

" 'Your supper was okay, wasn't it?'

" 'Yes.'

" 'I'm glad. You ain't never been in here to have your supper.'

" 'No.'

" 'I always like seeing you in here. They ain't nothing else good about this place.'

"I said nothing.

" 'My name's Martin, what's yours?'

"I didn't answer.

" 'I always wanted to know who you was.'

"I still didn't answer.

" 'You always like to know who you talking to, or looking at. I mean, if you like somebody.'

"No answer.

" 'You still there?'

" 'Yes, I'm still here,' I said so softly I almost didn't hear myself, but he must've heard me.

" 'I'm glad you still there,' he said. 'I thought you'd got up and gone.'

" 'No.'

" 'My name's Martin.'

"I still wouldn't tell him what my name was.

" 'I don't mean you no harm.'

"I wouldn't say anything. I just kept looking down at the table. I wouldn't even look at him. I felt as if tears were in my eyes, but I hoped he didn't see them. It was like I couldn't say nothing, Ursa, it was just like my mouth was there, but I just couldn't say nothing. I kept expecting him to be like the other mens was, and say real evil, 'You got a mouth, ain't you, bitch? I know you can talk,' but instead he was still soft. He said, 'I didn't come over here to mean you no harm, woman. I just wanted to talk to you.' That was the first time anybody called me woman. I didn't feel like a woman. I couldn't been more than your age when you left here. Naw, I didn't even feel like no woman and he called me one. I would've just stayed there, my eyes glued on that table. I know I would've just stayed there, till he left or something. I don't know. But all a sudden this ole woman come in selling these Jehovah Witness pamphlets and come over to him first. 'The Lord knows you guilty,' she said. I think that's what she said. He said, 'Yes, He does.' I don't know what else, because I put my money down on the table and got up and left. I could feel his eyes following me, like he wanted to push that ole woman away, but I could still hear her talking. Then I was out the door, and went on back home. I couldn't help feeling like I was saved from something, like Jesus had saved me from something. I went to bed real early that night. But still it was like something had got into me. Like my body or something knew what it wanted even if I didn't want no man. Cause I knew I wasn't lookin for none. But it was like it knew it wanted you. It was like my whole body knew it wanted you, and knew it would have you, and knew you'd be a girl. But something got into me after that night, though, Ursa. It was like my whole body knew. Just knew what it wanted, and I kept going back there. I told Mama and Grandmama that I had to work, you know, and I go there and eat my supper, and then I come home and eat supper again. My stomach got all stretched out too. I almost felt like I was getting a baby then. First two nights he wouldn't say nothing to me. Pretend like he wasn't even looking at me. I knew he was though. And I kept telling myself I wasn't looking for no man, I just wanted him to be my friend or something. You know, just somebody other than Mama and Gram I could go talk to sometime, you know what I mean. I wasn't lookin for no man, cause I didn't feel like no woman then. Sometimes even after I had you I still wouldn't feel like none. But then I just kept going there. It wasn't until bout the third or fourth night, he come and said something to me again, like he was getting up his nerve too.

" 'I wouldn't mean you no harm,' he said. Still that soft voice, almost like I really couldn't hear it now, or like I didn't want to hear it. 'I wouldn't mean you no harm, woman.'

"I think I mighta even been liking him calling me that, like men never did call women that before, or like that was just a special name for me, his special name for me.

" 'You ain't leavin again?' he asked.

" 'I haven't left,' I said. I didn't know whether he meant imaginary leavin or real leavin. But I was still sitting there.

" 'I want to walk you home. I'd like to walk you home tonight,' he said.

" 'I live kind of a distance. We live over in Bracktown.'

" 'You take the bus?'

" 'Yeah.'

" 'I ride you over there then.'

"I said nothing, but he took it to mean yes. Maybe it had meant yes.

" 'Who you live with?'

" 'My mama and my grandmama.'

" 'Maybe tha's why you seem like a old-fashioned girl.'

"I said nothing.

" 'I got to go over here and wait on these people. Don't leave now.'

"I said I wouldn't.

"I waited for him, and he stood waiting on the bus with me, and rode me home. He didn't even try to do nothing that first time. He didn't even ask me for a kiss. It was like we got along real well, like I wouldn't even believe you could get along that well with a man. But then I know it was something my body wanted, just something my body wanted. Naw. It just seem like I just keep telling myself that, and it's got to be something else. It's always something else, but it's easier if it's just that. It just always makes it easier. And then maybe he just wanted something else.

"He rode me home again, and then one night it had got kind of cold. You know, it was Indian summer and you never really could tell in the morning how it would be in the evening. I always took a sweater or jacket or something to work, but he didn't, cause he lived just right up the road, but, you know, riding me home all that way, he'd get cold, so he asked if he could go home and get his jacket first. He asked if I wanted to wait downstairs for him, but I said Naw, I said I'd go up. I guess I was thinking if I didn't it would be like saying that I didn't trust him. And then I was trusting him, and I was trusting myself too, because I really didn't think nothing would happen. But then he was getting his jacket, and then he all of a sudden touched my hand, and was talking about my hands, how I had nice long hands, and asked if I played piano, and asked if I minded if he touched me. Naw, I didn't mind, because I didn't mind it. Because I didn't think anything would happen, and I trusted myself, because I knew I wasn't looking for a man."

She stopped. I didn't ask her to go on. I knew she would go on when she was ready. She just kept sitting there for a long time. I just kept watching the side of her face, her mouth tightening again, the rows of plaits, the bun in the back, her profile. It was like I hadn't seen anyone so still as she'd suddenly gotten, more like when a movie freezes than in real life. Then the quivering started about her mouth again.

"It was like my whole body wanted you, Ursa. Can you understand that?"

"Yes, I can understand."

"I knew you was gonna come out a girl even while you was in me. Put my hand on my belly, and knew you was gonna be one of us. Little long-haired girl on my lap. You come out baldheaded though. They just kept looking at me, Mama and Gram. I knew they hated me then. Cause you come out all baldheaded. White skin before you got the little pigment you got now, and baldheaded. They hated me, but then your hair start to sprout, and got real long. I used to put a little ribbon on your head so people would know you was a girl. People didn't know whether you was a boy or a girl . . . I knew you'd be a girl. I knew my body would have a girl."

I said nothing.

She looked at me quickly, and then looked away again.

"He kept asking if he could touch me certain places, and I kept saying yes. And then all of a sudden it was like I felt the whole man in me, just felt the whole man in there. I pushed him out. It was like it was just that feeling of him in there. And nothing else. I hadn't even given myself time to feel anything else before I pushed him out. But he must have . . . I . . . still that memory, feeling of him in me. I wouldn't let myself feel anything. It was like a surprise. Like a surprise when he got inside. Just that one time. I didn't go see him anymore. I wouldn't even have my lunch there. Once he came to the depot and asked me why was I fighting him. I wouldn't say nothing to him. Then he just left me alone. He said he knew what I was now, and he could play that game too. I didn't know what he meant, but it made me feel bad. When I knew about you, Great Gram went and talked to him. I begged her not to, but he came and married me and then . . . he left me."

I wanted to ask if she would have left him, but I didn't. What I wanted to know now was if she had planned to leave him, but I couldn't bring myself to ask.

"Are you still there?"

I was silent.

"I went to see him only one time. He seen you. You was about two the last time he seen you, so I know you don't remember him."

"No."

"He was staying at some boarding house up in Cincinnati. I hadn't heard from him, and then he sent me this money. No letter, just this money and his address on the outside. I was mad at first, and then, Ursa, I didn't want him back or nothing. I even said my reason was to go give him his money back, cause I didn't need it, or wont it. When I got up there I just said I come to talk to him. Then I found out it was only just to get me up there. He knew when he sent that, I be up there. I was up there. He just stood in his door for a moment looking at me. He had on these khaki-colored pants, shirt on but chest all out anyway. I went in and he closed the door. He turned on me and first thing he said was, 'Bitch.' He said it again. 'Bitch.'

"I said, 'Don't hurt me.' I knew he was going to. I said, 'Help me, Martin, but don't hurt me. Just let me come here, and say hello, and ask you how you're doing. I just wonted to tell you things are all right with me and Ursa. I don't need the money.'

" 'Shit. Money's not how I helped you. I helped you that night, didn't I?' He held my arm. 'Didn't I?'

" 'You're hurting me.'

" 'I helped you that night.'

" 'No, you didn't, you hurt me.'

" 'I lived in that house long enough to know I helped you. How long was it? Almost two years, wasn't it? That's long enough for any man to know if he's helped. How could I have missed. I mean, the first time. The other times were all miss, weren't they, baby? They were all miss, weren't they?'

"He squeezed tighter. I kept trying to get away, but then he started slapping me, just slapping me all over the face. One time it was like he was going to go for some place else, like he was going to go straight for my cunt, or for my belly, or some place like that, but then he stopped himself, and just kept slapping me all over my face, twisting me, and slapping me all over my face. I didn't think I'd get out of there. I didn't think I would. I started to scream. And then I said, Naw, to myself. I said, Naw, I wasn't going to scream for no nigger, and having people coming up there and make me feel worse than I did already. I said, Naw, I wasn't going to scream for no nigger.

"But all of a sudden he just stopped. He just stopped and stood stone still. He hated me, Ursa. I know he did. I was holding myself all up on my face, and I know I was going to be black and blue all over, it hurt so bad. I was just hugging my face.

" 'Ain't I helped you, baby?' He was trying to grin, but it just made him look like the devil. 'Woman?'

"I didn't answer. I just kept hugging my face.

" 'Hurt, don't it?' he asked.

"I said nothing. I just wanted to get out of there. I didn't want him to do anything else, and it was like I was daring him not to touch me again, but I knew there wasn't nothing I could do if he did. I knew I wouldn't do nothing even if I could.

" 'What was you afraid of?' he asked.

"I said nothing.

" 'You could've let me. I know you could have let me. What were you afraid of, Correy?' He always called me Correy, you know.

"I still wouldn't say nothing. I never did tell him. I never would. I think he just thought I was just afraid of him being a man, or being too big, or too much for me or something. I never would tell him.

"He just let me go on to the door, then. Or I thought he was going to let me. He kept looking at me like he was hurt, and then when I tried to get around him to the door, he stood aside. But then all of a sudden he grabbed my pants. I had on these purple pants, the kind with the elastic waistband. He grabbed them by the waist, like when you're grabbing a child or something. He grabbed them and the elastic broke. I caught them before they fell down. He said he was sorry, but he didn't look like he was. I didn't bring anything with me, cause I was just going to see him, you know, and come on back home, so I didn't have anything. I was holding them up. I thought he would give me a pin or something but he didn't. He just stood looking at me, like he was real, real calm now, and then all at once the evil come back, and then he said, 'Get out.' He told me to get out. I ain't never seen a man look like that, Ursa. When you see a man look like that, you don't never forget it. It stay with you all your life. He told me to get on out of there and I did. He said, 'Go on down the street, lookin like a whore. I wont you to go on down the street, lookin like a whore.' I kind of looked at him, you know, and it was like I could see all that hurt there. He hadn't really softened, but I could still see all that hurt there. 'You took me bout as far as a woman can take a man without givin him nothing,' he said. 'Remember?' I went out. I didn't want to remember. I had to walk down the street, holding up my purple pants with one hand and holding my mouth with the other. My head was all hanging it hurt so bad, and I could feel it turning black and blue, and peoples was all watching. I know what they was thinking. The womens was looking at me all disgusted, and I was scared to borrow a pin offa somebody. Cause if I asked one of the mens for one, they would've thought I wonted something. This man leaning against this building kind of stood out and said, 'Baby, you know where Bud's Angel Bar is?' I just kept on walking. He said, 'Bitch, I ain't good enough for you, is I? I ain't good enough for you. Well, you ain't good enough for me neither.' I knew what he thought I was, but I just kept on walking."

I had leaned farther across the table, watching her. Just the side of her face was enough for me, she didn't even have to show me the rest, but she looked around and showed me the rest.

"I only went back to him once. He was staying at this boarding house, Ursa. All he did was start beating on me. He started beating on me."

I went over and put her head against my thighs.

"I carried him to the point where he ended up hating me, Ursa. And that's what I knew I'd keep doing. That's what I knew I'd do with any man."

"I'll walk you to the highway."

"You don't have to, Mama."

"I want to."

"Ursa."

"What, Mama?"

"I know about those other things you would never let me know."

I said nothing. She was telling me she knew about my own private memory.

"Do you want me to talk?"

"Sometime when you're back here and feel you have to."

"Awright."

She pulled her shawl around her tighter. I fingered my trade beads.

"You see all these colors in them, these formations?" I asked.

She looked at my neck, and touched them. We stopped walking for a moment.

"They form naturally," I said. "They just form naturally that way. No one paints them on."

"Those stripes too?"

"Yes."

She looked like she couldn't believe it, but I knew she did. She kept touching them for a time and then we started walking. We walked slowly.

"You didn't ask where your father is now, Ursa."

"Do you want to tell me?"

"No. I mean, I don't know."

We kept walking. We walked so slow it was almost like we weren't really walking. We had left early enough for me not to miss the bus, though, as if she had wanted to stand down there with me as long as possible before I had to get up on the bus, and she had to turn around and go back up to that house. The only thing that had changed in it was the kitchen, the old iron coal stove replaced with a gas one—the kind you used bottle gas from a tank outside the house, like people do in the country where there are no gas lines—and the old icebox replaced by a Frigidaire. She had moved the icebox into a corner and used it for storage space. And the old iron stove was still rusting in the backyard. The one they used to empty ashes from, lifting out those big iron rings in the top. That stove had always frighted me. When I was older, though, they'd make me take the tray out, and empty the ashes against the side of the road. The big bed was still in the middle room, except she had moved the trundle bed out of the front room, and put it in there too. I didn't know whether she slept in the big bed or the trundle one, and that wasn't something I felt I could ask her. It would have seemed ridiculous to an outsider, but to us I think it would have been a kind of prying she didn't want, or need. *They'd slept there before I did.* And in the front room that ageless china cabinet. The big one with all the good dishes and the silverware that was never taken out. I could never remember its ever having come out, even on holidays. The only time it was opened was to be dusted or polished. I'd never looked, but I think it had been imported from Brazil, or I used to think so. It was an expensive dark-mahogany thing, the best thing we had in the house. Great Gram used to be in charge of it at first, and then Grandmama, and now I guess Mama was. When I had gone through the house, it was still sparkling.

After a while, she began speaking again, hugging her shawl to her. It sounded almost as if she were speaking in pieces, instead of telling one long thing.

"After he come, they didn't talk to me about making generations anymore or about anything that happened with Corregidora, but Martin and me could hear them in there talking between theyselves. We'd be in the front room, and they'd be back in there in the bedroom, Great Gram telling Mama how Corregidora wouldn't let her see some man because he was too black." Mama kept talking until it wasn't her that was talking, but Great Gram. I stared at her because she wasn't Mama now, she was Great Gram talking: "He wouldn't let me see him, cause he said he was too black for me. He liked his womens black, but he didn't wont us with no black mens. It wasn't color cause he didn't even wont us with no light black mens, cause there was a man down there as light as he was, but he didn't even wont us with him, cause there was one girl he caught with him, and had her beat, and sold the man over to another plantation, cause I think he just wont to get rid of him anyway. Cause Corregidora himself was looking like a Indian—if I said that to him I have my ass off—so that this light black man looked more like a white man than he did, so I just think he wont any excuse to get rid of him. I don't even know how he got him. He didn't buy him himself, I think he just come in with a load of other mens they wont to work out in the fields, cause he had cane, you know. But anyway he wouldn't let me see him, cause he said a black man wasn't nothing but a waste of pussy, and wear me out when it came to the other mens. He didn't send nothing but the rich mens in there to me, cause he said I was his little gold pussy, his little gold piece, and it didn't take some of them old rich mens no time, and then I still be fresh for him. But he said he didn't wont no waste on nothing black. Some of them womens he had just laying naked, and just sent trash into them. But some of us he called hisself cultivating us, and then didn't send nothing but cultivated mens to us, and we had these private rooms, you know. But some of these others, they had to been three or four or five whores fucking in the same room. But then if we did something he didn't like he might put us in there and send trash into us, and then we be catching everything then. So after that, first time he just talked to me real hard, said he didn't wont no black bastard fucking me, he didn't wont no black bastard fucking all in his piece. He was real mad. He grab hold of me down between my legs and said he didn't wont nothing black down there. He said if he just catch me fucking something black, they wouldn't have no pussy, and he wouldn't have none neither. And then he was squeezing me all up on my pussy and then digging his hands up in there. We was up in his room. That's where he always bring me when he wont to scold me about something, or fuck with me. Him and his wife was living in separated rooms then. Then he was just digging all up in me till he got me where he wonted me and then he just laid me down on that big bed of his and started fucking me . . .

"Any of them, even them he had out in the fields, if he wonted them, he just ship their own husbands out of bed, and get in there with them, but didn't nothing happen like what happened over on that other plantation, cause I guess that other plantation served as a warning, cause they might wont your pussy, but if you do anything to get back at them, it'll be your life they be wonting, and then they make even that some kind of a sex show, all them beatings and killings wasn't nothing but sex circuses, and all them white peoples, mens, womens, and childrens crowding around to see . . .

"Naw, he said he wouldn't've been nothing but a waste of my pussy, cause he said my pussy bring gold. But what was funny after that they kept claiming he did something. Not Corregidora, but this black man. I was only talking to him once, all Corregidora did was seen us talking, and I guess he figure the next step was we be down in the grass or something. I don't know, but they said he did something,

and they were goin to beat him real bad. He was young
too, young man, so he run away. When somebody run away,
it almost mean you can do whatever you wont to with
them. I think he woulda run away anyway, cause he had
this dream, you know, of running away and joining up with
them renegade slaves up in Palmares, you know. I kept
telling him that was way back before his time, but he
wouldn't believe me, he said he was going to join up with
some black mens that had some dignity. You know, Palmares, where these black mens had started their own town,
escaped and banded together. I said the white men had
killed all of them off but he wouldn't believe me. He said
that was what his big dream was, to go up there and join
all these other black mens up there, and have him a woman,
and then come back and get his woman and take her up
there, but he had to find his way first, and know exactly
where he was going. I said he couldn't know where he was
going because Palmares was way back two hundred years
ago, but he said Palmares was now. But they claimed he
did something, and he had to leave before he planned to.
Wasn't nothing but seventeen or eighteen. This ole man
said he told him to rub garlic on his feet so the hounds
wouldn't smell him, but he said the boy must've forgot to.
We was all praying for him, though. They sent this whole
mob of mens out after him. You know, they didn't need no
mob for just one person. Mob and hounds. So they can have
the hounds to smell out nigger blood, cause they trained
them to do that. But it was only because Corregidora
thought he'd been fooling with me when he hadn't, or that
we'd been fooling with each other, cause all that was all
uncalled-for. Sometimes I would be a little bold with him,
little bolder than the others, cause I know I was the piece
he wonted the most, so I said, 'He wasn't after my pussy.
He ain't been after my pussy. He even too young to know

I got one.' 'Ain't no nigger on this place too young to know you got one, way I got them trained,' he said. He moved away from me, then he moved back toward me. He must've been fucking me while they was chasing after *him*. But maybe he did the right thing to run anyway, because maybe if he had stayed there, the way Corregidora was looking when he seen us talking he might've had him beat dead. I ain't never seen him look like that, cause when he send them white mens in there to me he didn't look like that, cause he be nodding and saying what a fine piece I was, said I was a fine speciment of a woman, finest speciment of a woman he ever seen in his life, said he had tested me out hisself, and then they would be laughing, you know, when they come in there to me. Cause tha's all they do to you, was feel up on you down between your legs see what kind of genitals you had, either so you could breed well, or make a good whore. Fuck each other or fuck them. Tha's the first thing they would think about, cause if you had somebody who was a good fucker you have plenty to send out in the field, and then you could also make you plenty money on the side, or inside. But he was up there fucking me while they was out chasing *him*. 'Don't let no black man fool with you, do you hear? I don't wont nothing black fucking with my pussy.' I kept saying I wouldn't. 'I don't wont nothing black trying to fuck you, do you hear that?' 'Yes, I hear.' Let his own color mess with me all they wont to. Sometimes I used to think he even wonted to be in there watching, but out of respect for them, not me, he wouldn't. Yes, tha's just how I was feeling, while he was up there jumping up and down between my legs they was out there with them hounds after that boy. Wasn't nothing but seventeen. Couldn't've been more than seventeen or eighteen. And he had this dream he told me about. That was all he wanted me for, was to tell me about this dream. He must've trusted me a lot, though, cause I could've been one of them to run back to Corregidora with it. But I wouldn't. It was because he seen us out there talking. I wouldn't even go tell him, cause I would've been seen telling him. And I kept feeling all that time he was running, he kept thinking I'd told something when I didn't. And then there I was kept crying out, and ole Corregidora thinking it was because he was fucking so good I was crying. 'Ain't nobody do it to you like this, is it?' I said, 'Naw.' I just kept saying Naw, and he just kept squeezing on my ass and fucking. And then somehow it got in my mind that each time he kept going down in me would be that boy's feets running. And then when he come, it meant they caught him . . .

"When they come back, they said they lost the boy at the river. They said they got to the river they didn't see him no more. We was all glad. We didn't show it, but the rest of us was all glad and rejoicing inside. But you know what happened? Three days after that somebody seen him floating on the water. What happened was they chased him as far as the river and he just jumped in and got drownded. Cause they didn't know nothing till three days after that when he rose . . .

"Corregidora must've done some rejoicing then. He didn't show it but he must've had it all inside. Ole man kept telling me if the boy had just remembered to rub garlic on his feet, the bloodhounds wouldn't've been able to follow. I asked him if he ever tried it. He said, Naw, but he heard of folks that did. I asked him where was they. He said they was gone. He didn't know where to, but they must've made it, cause didn't nobody bring them back."

She quit talking, and looked over at me suddenly, Mama again: "They just go on like that, and then get in to talking about the importance of passing things like that down. I've heard that so much it's like I've learned it off by heart. But then with him there they figured they didn't have to tell me no more, but then what they didn't realize was they was telling Martin too ..."

It was as if she had *more* than learned it off by heart, though. It was as if their memory, the memory of all the Corregidora women, was her memory too, as strong with her as her own private memory, or almost as strong. But now she was Mama again.

"One day after we'd been married, I don't know, maybe six months. (He had come into the house to live, you know. Not on account of hisself but me. I kept saying I couldn't not help them out, and if we didn't live there, I couldn't help us and them too. He said he'd help us, all I had to do was worry about them. I said something about how little he was making. Naw, it was almost like he moved in that house out of anger, not for me, but for anger.) Well, he had gone fishing one day, but when he came back, though, instead of coming around to the front where I was, he went around the back to the kitchen and put them in a big pan of water, and then he was gonna come around to the front and have me cut them up and fry them. Well, what happened is he must've started through their room and there she was, sitting on that bed in there powdering up under her breasts. I don't know if she seen him or not—this was your grandmama—but she just kept powdering and humming, cause when I started through there, there she was powdering, and looking down at her breasts, and lifting them up and powdering under them, and there he was just standing in the door with his arms spread up over the door, and sweat showing through his shirt, just watching her. I don't know what kind of expression he had on his face. His lips was kind of smiling, but his eyes wasn't. He seen me and he just kept standing there. I was looking at Mama and then looking up at him, and after he seen me the first time he just kept looking at her. She was acting like she didn't know we was there, but I know she had to know. He was just standing there like he was hypnotized or something. I know she knew. She knew it, cause they both knew he wasn't getting what he wanted from me. Cause you know with them in there, I couldn't. I'd let him rub me down there. I kept telling him it was because they were in there that I wouldn't. But . . . even if they hadn't been. There she was just sitting there lifting up her breasts. I don't know when it was she decided she'd let him know she seen him, but then all a sudden she set the box of powder down and looked up. Her eyes got real hateful. First she looked at me, then she looked at him. 'You black bastard, watching me. What you doing watching me, you black bastard?' She still had her breasts all showing and just cussing at him. He started over there where she was, but I got between them. 'Martin, don't.' He just kept looking at me, like it was me he was hating, but it was her he was calling a half-white heifer. Her powder and him sweating all up under his arms, and me holding him. She kept calling him a nasty black bastard, and he kept calling her a half-white heifer.

" 'Messing with my girl, you ain't had no right messing with my girl.'

" 'I'ma come over there and mess with your ass the next time you show it,' he said, but then I got him in the kitchen, and there was them fish in that pan a water he had waiting for me to clean. He pushed me away from him, and grabbed them fish and started cutting them up hisself. 'What do we have to do, go up under the house?' he kept asking me. 'What do we have to do, go up under the house?'

" 'Please, Martin.'

"He just kept grabbing those fish and cutting them up.

"When I came back through the house, Mama rolled her

eyes at me. 'Messing with my girl, he ain't had no bit of right.'

"After that, whenever Martin wanted to get from one part of the house to the next, he'd go around the house ... But she just kept acting like she didn't even know he was there."

She was quiet again, and then she said, "They had us sleeping in the narrow old trundle bed in the front room, the one you was sleeping in afterwards. I kept telling him it was because they were in there I wouldn't, but then that time they weren't there he wanted to take me in *their* bed ..."

I didn't ask her whether she had let him. That was something she didn't have to tell me.

When we got to the highway, Mama took my arm.

"I think what really made them dislike Martin was because he had the nerve to ask them what I never had the nerve to ask."

"What was that?"

"How much was hate for Corregidora and how much was love."

I said nothing. She squeezed my arm. "I'll try to pretend you're okay until you tell me different," she said.

"I'm okay, Mama."

She kept looking at me. I didn't like the way she was looking. I wanted to ask what about her now, how lonely was *she*. She'd told me about *then*, but what about *now*. Shortly after Grandmama died, she had written me a letter saying that Mr. Floyd had started to get sweet on her, talking about how he wanted to court her, but she said she hadn't let him. She said he could just stay across that road, cause all he really wanted to do was to move out of that trailer, and into *her* house, and probably bring his mama with him. I hadn't known whether to believe her or not, because I knew too many of my own excuses when men came to the piano, and then Logan—the man Max hired to see to it that men don't bother me—was my best excuse. I could just give him that "he's bothering me" look, and he'd put the man out.

After a while, Mama squeezed my arm again. She kept hold of it until the bus came and she put me on. "Do you know me any better now?" she asked. I only smiled at her. She stayed standing there until the bus pulled off. She didn't let me see her walk back to the house.

I leaned back against the seat and closed my eyes. Then suddenly it was like I was remembering something out of a long past. I was a child, drowsy, thinking I was sleeping or dreaming. It was a woman and a man's voice, both whispering.

"No."

"Why don't you come?"

"No."

"What are you afraid of?"

"I'm not. I'm just not going with you."

"Why do you keep fighting me? Or is it yourself you keep fighting?"

I drifted back into sleep. I never heard that man's voice again.

I was thinking that now that Mama had gotten it all out, her own memory—at least to me anyway—maybe she and *some man* . . . But then, I was thinking, what had I done about my *own* life?

III

I couldn't have been more than ten the year the Melrose woman committed suicide. Mama had come into the house. Gram said something to her and then they started hushing each other because I was in the room. I saw the way they was looking, but Mama sent me back in the kitchen to light the oven because she was going to bake some rolls for dinner. I went back in the kitchen. They didn't think I could hear them, but I could. We had one of them three-room, straight-back shotgun houses. They was in the front room, and with just one room in between us, I could hear them. When I finished lighting the stove, I just sat down at the kitchen table and listened.

"Yeah, they found her over in Hawkins' alley," Mama was saying.

"Anybody know why yet?"

"They thought it must've been some man, you know, got her pregnant or something, but she wasn't pregnant."

"Had to been some man," Gram said. "I ain't never known a woman take her life less it was some man."

"I reckon," Mama said. She sounded weary. I didn't hear them say anything else, and finally Mama said she was going back in the kitchen and start supper. I put my head down on the table, so she wouldn't see my eyes.

It wasn't until later that I knew what they were talking

about. I was down at Mr. Deak's store, and him and these men were talking. They weren't like Mama and Gram. They didn't care if I was there or not. Mama had sent me down for some corn meal. I thought it had happened in Bracktown, but it wasn't Bracktown, it was up in Versailles that it happened, but the girl was from Bracktown —one of Mr. Melrose's girls. She was in her twenties.

"Melrose is up there now," Mr. Deak was saying. "Her mama is all to pieces. He told her to stay here, and he go take care of it. They gon move her body down here. But you know why he didn't wont Miz Melrose there, because he gon try to find out what man's responsible, buddy, it's gon be some fireworks in Versailles."

Mr. Deak was a little dark man who wore suspenders all the time, and stood with his thumbs under his suspenders, not up near his chest, but down near his waist. He must've been in his twenties, but I thought he was old then.

"You ain't forgot what your mama wanted, did you, missy?" he said to me.

"Naw, sir." I went and got the corn meal. I didn't take it over to the counter, I just stayed standing there.

The other man started talking. "How her daddy gonna find out, and the whole police couldn't?"

"A daddy got ways the police ain't. Anway, she wasn't nothing but a nigger woman to the police. You know they ain't gon take they time to find out nothing about a nigger woman. Somebody go down there and file a complaint, they write it down, all right, while you standing there, but as soon as you leave, they say, 'Here, put it in the nigger file.' That mean they get to it if they can. And most times they can't. Naw, they don't say put it in the nigger file, they say put it in the nigger *woman* file, which mean they ain't gon never get to it . . . You know, John Willie ain't gon do nothing. But her daddy, now, that's something different.

You heard about the shot heard round the world. They gon be some rumbling over here in Bracktown when Mr. Melrose find that man."

"Maybe it wasn't no man, maybe it was just she went crazy."

"Naw, it was a man. I bet my eyeteeth it was a man."

Mr. Deak looked at me again, this time real hard, and I handed him the money for the meal, and ran out the door.

"Did you hear what happened to that Melrose woman?" I asked May Alice. She was my girl friend. She was a couple of years older than me, though, and had already started bleeding. She called it bleeding, so I had started calling it bleeding. Before then I had been taught to call it monthly or time of month. They told me about it when I was nine. They wouldn't have told me that early, but I'd found some of Mama's bloody sheets and had started screaming and crying, and they couldn't convince me that mama wasn't sick until they told me about it. When I told May Alice, she'd laughed, and every since that, she would start pointing out people and saying, "She bleeds." At first I had liked "monthly" but then I had started liking her word better. I hadn't started bleeding yet, but May Alice said I would start in a few years. She said she had started early, though, and sounded like she was bragging. She said it was a good thing I'd had that scare then, because if they hadn't told me, and I'd seen all that blood in my bloomers, I would have had a bigger scare. She said she knew this girl who hadn't been told and when she saw all that blood she thought something was wrong with her, but was even too scared to tell her mama, and went down in the basement and kept trying to wipe the blood off, but it just kept coming, and she thought she was dying or something. Then May Alice laughed at me again.

"She wasn't a woman. She wasn't any older than my sister," May Alice said now.

"Your sister's married, ain't she?"

"That don't make her a woman. Anyway, Mama keeps telling her it's time for her to start acting like a woman. She might've had it in her, but that don't make her no woman."

"Had what in her?"

"Dick, silly."

"What?"

"Her husband's thing. A man's got something different from a girl."

"I know that."

"You don't act like it."

"I ain't seen one, but I know what it looks like."

"How?"

"I don't know."

"Because we was watching Mr. Trumbo's dick get hard through his pants, and I told you. You don't remember nothing."

"I remember."

"Well, just because somebody had it in them, don't make them no woman. I had it in me, and I ain't no woman."

"How you have it in you?"

"I just did, that's all. I opened my legs, and Harold put it in me. He said, 'Open your legs up, May Alice,' and I did. I played like I didn't know what he was going to do, but I did. Then he put his thing in me, and my pussy got all bloody."

"You said you already bleed."

"I do, but that's not the only kind of bleeding a woman, I mean a girl, have to put up with. The first time a man sticks it in you, you bleed."

"Does it hurt?"

"It does for a little while, and then it feels good."

"Naw it don't."

"Yes, it does."

"How can it feel good if it hurts."

"I said it hurts for a little while, and then all the hurting goes, and then it feels good."

"I don't believe you."

"You will. Rate you going, you probly be my sister's age, but you'll say, May Alice told me it would feel good."

"Naw I won't. I'll say May Alice told me a story."

She just laughed.

When we were older—or maybe I should say when I was older—May Alice always seemed the same age to me; I was about twelve myself then, no, I was thirteen, because I'd just started getting my period—I was in the six grade and she was in the eighth, but we had recess at the same time, and I saw her and Harold leave the playground and go over in Mr. Jouett's wheat field. Harold came back first, and then she came back and came over where I was.

"May Alice, you going to have a baby if you don't quit."

"Did Miss Smoot see us?"

"I don't know. I don't think she was looking."

"You know what'll happen if you don't quit," I said again.

She looked angry at first, and then she kind of laughed a little. "I been trying to, but then it gets so you can't help it. You'll find out."

I kind of frowned. She was always mentioning the fact that she'd been having it and I hadn't, like when we were younger and she would keep saying, "I got a bigger hole than you got," and asking me if I wanted to see it. I said, "Naw."

"I'll show it to you if you show me yours," she said.

"Naw."

"Reason I got a bigger hole than you got is cause Harold been in me."

"Harold can't get in you. You ain't got no door."

"Yes, I do, cause I got one down between my legs."

Then when I first started bleeding, I tried to get back at her. I said, "You said it would be red. It looks like chocolate." "It'll get red," she told me, and it did.

"Anyway," she went on now, "once you had it in you, it seems like you have to keep having it in you. I heard Mama talking about this woman that didn't have it done to her and went crazy. You got to have it in you, or you go crazy."

"You lying."

"Naw I ain't. Mama said this girl, there was this man that used to come and visit her mama, and her mama never would let her do nothing, and then this man left her house, and went walking down the street, and this girl broke loose, and ran down the street after him, and tried to rape him, right there on the sidewalk. They put her in the asylum after that."

I kept saying she was lying, and she kept saying naw she wasn't neither. Then Harold came over by us, and he was grinning. I told May Alice I had to go inside.

I never did tell her about that time I was home by myself and Harold and some more boys came and was standing outside the kitchen door wanting to get in, and I wouldn't let them in.

"Let us in, Ursa," Harold had said. "Let us in so we can give you a baby. Don't you want a baby?"

They kept knocking on the door. I wouldn't let them in the kitchen, so they went around to the front, but that was locked too.

"Henry said when you was five you let him see your pussy," Harold said.

"I ain't five now."

"He said you let him feel all up in your ass."

"Naw I didn't."

"Open the door so we can get some. Don't you want a baby?"

I was in the bathroom when May Alice came in.

"Why'd you leave? Harold says you don't like him."

I said nothing. I was thinking of that time we had gone through the cut-off, May Alice and me, and Harold and those boys were there again. Harold had gone over to May Alice and the other boys were after me, but May Alice had thrown rocks at them. "Don't let them get Urs," she'd said. "Harold, make them leave." When the other boys were gone, she and Harold got over in the grass. They were rolling like they were playing at first, and then I knew what they were doing. They hadn't even told me to turn my head.

"What's wrong, Urs?"

"You know what'll happen if you don't stop."

"I can take care of myself," she said, then she stuck her tongue out at me, and left.

I didn't even know what she saw in him, except that day we had a dance at school and he asked me to slow-dance, and he kept getting real close to me, and he felt real hot down between his legs. I didn't know anybody could feel that hot. When he asked me to dance again, I wouldn't dance with him. He went over and said something to some boys, and these boys were standing over in the corner, looking at me, laughing. No one else asked me to dance that evening.

"We did it again last night," May Alice said.

We were on the stairs going up to class. She had a torn place in the hem of her skirt. „

"May Alice, you better quit."

She said nothing.

"He ought to quit if you won't," I said.

"You know a boy won't quit."

"Why not?"

She laughed. "Anyway," she said, "they be after it till you tell them to stop. But then after you start giving them some, you wouldn't feel right to tell them to stop. I mean, you wouldn't feel you had any right to tell them to stop."

"I would."

"Who you gave some to?"

I said nothing. She turned to go in her class. I kept on walking.

There was a boy at school who used to rub up against girls. Once when it was crowded and we were all going to the cafeteria he rubbed up against me. I wouldn't hardly eat for a whole week, thinking he'd given me a baby, even though I knew from May Alice that you couldn't get them unless you had it in you. I wouldn't eat because I thought starving myself would get rid of it. Mama had kept saying, don't you want such and such a thing, you better eat, Ursa, and I would keep saying I wasn't hungry. And then she had said, "You die if you don't eat." I don't know how long I could have kept it up, but then May Alice's own scare drove me back to eating again. Yes, she had had a scare before she got really pregnant. She thought she was pregnant and kept asking me whether she should take a coat hanger like she heard some people did. I'd told her it would probably ruin her more doing that than if she went on and had the baby. She wasn't even acting like she used to, like she would act when she was so sure of herself. She said she knew all about having babies but not how to get rid of them. I asked her didn't she know how to keep from having them. She said, Yeah, but Harold was getting so now he was getting careless, and I asked her wasn't she getting careless too. She said it was just that now she didn't like to ask him to use something, and didn't want to tell him to pull out.

But then her period had finally come that time. It was the next time that it didn't. At first she kept telling me it was only because she'd been eating too much. "I've just been eating too much, I've just been eating too much, that's all," she kept telling me. But that day when she couldn't tell me that anymore, I skipped class with her and we spent the whole afternoon sitting down in the wheat field, and she kept hugging me and crying, and hugging me, and saying why couldn't I have been Harold and then nothing would have happened. I didn't know what she was talking about then. She just kept hugging me.

She said her mama found out because she got suspicious when she'd stopped finding blood in her underwear when she did the wash. She'd tried to tell her that she'd washed it out herself, but her mama said she never did before, and took her down to Midway and had Dr. Roach examine her. May Alice said she wouldn't even look at the doctor, she just kept rolling her eyes at him. She said it wasn't like when you were making love or playing doctor, when a man opened your legs and looked at you down there. She said it was the most embarrassing thing a woman could go through. She said all she did was roll her eyes at him. Then she said the next week when her mama went to find out the results, she came back home and slapped her, and said the only reason she didn't keep slapping her was because she didn't want to be responsible for anything happening to the baby, and keep her from paying the consequences she deserved to pay.

May Alice kept asking me to go tell Harold she was sorry, but I wouldn't. I said she shouldn't be sorry, he should be. But she just kept telling me to go tell Harold she was sorry, like it was her fault.

"He won't come to see me," she would say. "Ursie, go tell him I'm sorry. He's mad at me. I know he is."

"He ain't got no right to be mad at you," I said. "You should be mad at him."

"Go tell him I'm sorry, please."

"I can't tell him that."

"Ursie, please."

I finally got up enough nerve to go tell Harold she said she was sorry.

"It ain't me, it's my mama," he said, and got away from me real quick.

The next time she asked me to tell him she was sorry, I wouldn't.

I was back in her room with her when Harold's mama came to talk to her mama. They had started to say something, but then May Alice's mama said why didn't they go out in the yard and talk, because she knew we could hear. May Alice and me went in the front room and watched them from the window, but couldn't hear anything.

"His mama just got out of the hospital having a baby herself," she said.

"How you know?"

She said nothing, then she said, "When we did it the last time, he was home by hisself. She was in the hospital then. His daddy hadn't come home from work yet."

I said nothing. I just kept looking out at the two mamas talking, and wondered what it would be like if one of them was mine, and the idea frightened me.

"What are they going to do?" I asked.

"His mama sho is ugly," she said, instead of answering. "She's the only one in the family that's ugly. I don't see what Harold's daddy see in her anyway, except but she's probably real good in the bed."

I said nothing. I just kept staring out at the two women. When I got back home, Mama had found out about May

Alice's pregnancy. I hadn't told her, but I guessed by now the word had started slipping out.

"I told you not to have nothing to do with that girl. I told your grandmama I used to see her back in that grass back there. Young as she is too. Girl like that, it ain't nothing but shaking hands. Let her see how hard he's gon be shaking her hand now. Nothing but shaking hands. I reckon you listen to me now, Ursa."

I said nothing.

"You hear me, don't you?"

"Yes, ma'am."

I didn't see May Alice again until she had had the baby. She was in the hospital, in a room with all these other women whose stomachs were swollen out. I almost hadn't gone in when I saw the rest of them, but May Alice had seen me, and I wouldn't have felt right if I'd turned around and left.

"I didn't think you liked me no more."

"I like you, May Alice."

"Harold don't."

I just stood there. She told me I could sit on the bed, but I wouldn't. I kept looking at her because I didn't want to have to look at the other women.

"You looking at me so funny," she said, and tried to laugh.

"Naw I'm not."

She said nothing, and then she started telling me how pretty the baby was.

"Did you go see him?"

"Naw, they wasn't showing the babies when I got here."

"Aw. Maybe you get to see him tomorrow."

I said, "Yes," but I knew I didn't want to come back.

May Alice started smiling.

"What you smiling at?"

"It's a hurt that feels good too. I mean afterwards. You remember what I told you and you wouldn't believe me."

I nodded.

She started telling me how the baby felt coming out from between her legs.

"Don't tell me about that." I stepped away from the bed.

"When it happens to you, you'll be wanting to talk about it too."

"Naw, I won't, cause it ain't gonna happen to me."

"Don't be such a baby," she said. "When you started bleeding you still acted like a baby. I bet when you have your first man in you, you'll still act like you do now. Like a baby."

I turned away and ran out. I didn't want to see May Alice anymore.

I remember when I got home I ran up to Mr. Deak's store.

"Mr. Deak, whatever happened to Mr. Melrose?"

"Honey, that ain't nothing for you to hear."

It wasn't until I was about fifteen that I learned from reading back papers in the school library that him and some man got in a fight at the Spider Web—not the Spider where I was to work later, but the old Spider Web that was long since torn down—and that he had either shot or knifed the man, the paper wasn't too sure which. But now Mr. Melrose was in jail, and the police had claimed they still didn't know whether the man he had shot or knifed had had anything to do with his daughter. They still didn't know why she'd killed herself. John Willie, of the police department, had said, "There's some things them people just won't let be our business no matter how hard we try. We still asking around though." I felt like going down to the county jail to ask Mr. Melrose, but I knew Mama wouldn't let me, and even if I had gotten in there, I figured Mr. Melrose would either think I was crazy, or resent me for meddling. I don't think anything ever worked me up so much as that woman, and I hadn't really known her, or paid that much attention to her, just seen her, because she was twenty-some years old, and a woman, and I was only a kid, but somehow I'd kept tying her and May Alice together. I don't know why I did. And it was always May Alice laying up there in that alley.

I never went to see May Alice no more, and then finally she and her mama moved to Georgetown, Kentucky. I'd seen her a few weeks after she got back with the baby, though. She'd stayed in for the first few weeks. I don't know if it was because her mama believed in those forty days or felt ashamed. But as soon as May Alice did come out, I saw her. It was hard not to see anybody in Bracktown. I was going across the railroad track to go to Mr. Deak's store, and she was coming back from there.

"Why you hate me?" she asked.

She still had on one of her maternity dresses even though her stomach wasn't big anymore.

"I don't hate you."

"Yes, you do. You ain't been to see me."

"I didn't know you'd be having company."

"You know you could come. You my best friend, ain't you?"

I said nothing.

"Did what I said in the hospital make you mad?"

I shook my head.

"Yes it did. That's why, ain't it?"

"Naw."

"Why then?"

I said nothing.

"All right. Hell," she said. "I ain't gonna stand here. Least you could do for somebody is tell 'em why you don't like 'em. Shit. You ain't nothing *but* a baby. I was just talking, thought maybe I could help you. Even if a man stuck a dick as big as a tree up in you, you wouldn't get help. All you like to do is watch."

"I don't."

"You was, wasn't you?"

She started laughing. I wanted to say something real nasty to her, but instead I ran across the railroad track without looking. For a long time after that, I would just sit up trying to think of things that would have sent *her* running. Once Mama came by while I was whispering something and slapped me. "Who taught you that? I ain't taught you that." I just kept looking at her. But after that day, though, me and May Alice didn't speak to each other, and then finally her and her mama moved. I don't know if her father ever knew about her baby because she said he lived up in New Jersey, where he could get a job, and would send them home money. I just wondered why they moved to Georgetown and didn't go up to New Jersey somewhere.

When I first had people liking my singing, it was down at that place that was more somebody's house than a restaurant. When Mama found out she came and got me.

"I ain't gon have you singing no devil music. Me over there sitting up in church trying to praise God, and you over at Preston's singing to the devil."

"What about Grandmama's old blues records? You didn't say nothing to her."

She didn't answer, then she said, "That ain't the devil coming out of your own mouth."

I told her she didn't have to embarrass me, pulling me out of Preston's like that, with all them people watching. She coulda just told me. She said she ain't never known no

Corregidora to behave with just telling. That was when I told her I wasn't no Corregidora. She just kept looking at me, and then she told me she better not catch me down there at Preston's no more or else I have the devil coming out of my behind as well as my mouth.

We just kept having riffs like that until I just got on the bus and came to the city. I read in the paper where they needed somebody at Happy's. When I got there I just kept standing outside the place, afraid to go in. There was this man that come by, and just stood there and watched me. I was almost as afraid of him as I was to go in.

He said, "Whose woman is you?"

I wouldn't look at him.

" 'Whose woman is you' I asked."

I still wouldn't answer.

"You got your bitch on today, ain't you?"

I stood there.

"I said, 'Ain't you got your bitch on today?' "

I think I got up enough nerve to go inside just because I wanted to get rid of him. Tadpole liked me right off, and I got the job.

"I bet you some man's good woman, ain't you?"

Tadpole had put the man out.

When I first saw Mutt I was singing a song about a train tunnel. About this train going in the tunnel, but it didn't seem like they was no end to the tunnel, and nobody knew when the train would get out, and then all of a sudden the tunnel tightened around the train like a fist. Then I sang about this bird woman, whose eyes were deep wells. How she would take a man on a long journey, but never return him.

Mutt kept looking at me. Somehow I thought he would come up and say something to me like the other men did who'd looked at me like that. I hadn't wanted them or anything, but they'd come. His look was like theirs and somehow different too. He kept coming into the place, and somehow, even though he'd never come up to me, and I'd never said anything to him, he got to be the man I was singing to. I would look at him when I began a song, and somehow I would be looking at him when I ended it. He kept coming into the place, and then one night he got up and asked me to join him at his table.

"Where did you get those songs?"

I'd sung the ones about the tunnel and the bird woman again.

"I made them up."

"They real nice. I like the way you sing."

He asked me what I wanted to drink. I said beer.

He looked surprised. "Nothing harder? You give the impression of liking bourbon."

"No, that's all I drink."

He grinned. "You not such a hard woman. You try to sing hard, but you not hard. I bet you try to talk hard, too, don't you?"

I didn't answer.

"You don't have to say nothing," he said.

The waitress brought me my beer, and him his whiskey. We said nothing for a while and he kept looking at me. I didn't look at him, and then I looked at him. "What?" I asked.

"I feel I know you from way back," he said, and then he started telling me about some trouble he got in when he was back home. He didn't tell me where home was, and I didn't ask.

"I was wrong, though, but I got off."

"How could you get off if you was wrong?" I asked.

"Cause he wouldn't a did nothing to me, judge wouldn't."

"Why?"

"On account of him and my daddy. Yeah, cause he knew if it wasn't for my daddy he wouldn't even be the judge down there. You know, my daddy worked for him. It's a little town. You know how in these little towns they even make a farmer a judge. They made Judge Tackett a judge and he didn't have nothing but a ninth-grade education. 'You have to be a lawyer to be a judge,' that's what my daddy told him. Judge Brackman's a lawyer, you know. Well, he was running for election, and my daddy said, 'You a lawyer. Why don't you tell them you got to be a lawyer to be a judge.' So that's what Judge Brackman did, said you got to be a lawyer to be a judge. He used it in his campaign speech, and he got elected too. Tha's why now anything I do there, I can get off of it."

"Anything?"

"Wasn't nothing but a traffic charge," he said with a smile. "I ain't a bad man. I can be hard sometime, but I ain't bad." He looked at me carefully for a moment. "Naw, you ain't no hard woman."

"I know my way around," I said. I don't even know why I said it, it was just like it came out. I wasn't even sure it was true. It was just that I was singing in a place where a woman would know her way around.

"Do you?" he asked.

I drank my beer.

"My name's Mutt."

"Oh."

"I thought you might like to know who you talking to."

"Yes. I'm . . ."

"I know who you are."

I smiled, still holding my glass.

"You scared of me, ain't you?"

"Why do you say that?"

"The way you look at me."

"Naw, I'm not scared."

I drank some more beer and put the glass down. I was thinking of how the first night I saw him in there his hair hadn't been combed, and every night after that, he'd combed his hair. I smiled.

"What you smiling at?"

"Nothing," I said, still smiling.

He smiled. "You'll get over that," he said.

"What?"

"Being afraid of me."

He looked around him.

"This ain't really a good place for a woman."

I said I liked it.

He didn't say anything else about it, then. It wasn't until later that he started saying other things. He was a big man, not heavy, but tall big.

"I like you," he said. "I got some Della Reese records. She's my woman. I like you though. I mean, I don't just like your singing, I like you too."

I said nothing.

After a while, he said very quietly, "You got somebody?"

I said, "No."

He smiled a little. "Yeah, she's my woman. Her and Ella. The rest of em can't do nothing for me. Now the Lady Billie she . . ."

When I told Mutt about Corregidora, it was before we got married. I hadn't gone to his apartment and he hadn't been to mine, but now we had gotten so he would come into my dressing room and we would talk there. He said he only knew one thing about when his people were slaves, but that it was enough for him. I asked him what was it. He said that his great-grandfather—he guessed great-grandfather—had worked as a blacksmith, hiring hisself out, and bought his freedom, and then he had bought his wife's freedom. But then he got in debt to these men, and he didn't have any money, so they come and took his wife. The courts judged that it was legal, because even if she was his wife, and fulfilled the duties of a wife, he had bought her, and so she was also his property, his slave. He said his great-grandfather had just gone crazy after that. "You can imagine how he must of felt."

I nodded, but said nothing.

"Don't look like that, Ursa," he had said and pulled me toward him. "Whichever way you look at it, we ain't them."

I didn't answer that, because the way I'd been brought up, it was almost as if I was.

"We're not, Ursa."

I had stepped back suddenly.

"What did you step back for, woman? I wasn't going to bite you. What in the hell did you step back for?"

He was looking at me with more hurt than anger. But when I came back toward him, he acted like he didn't want me then. Said he was going out and get himself a drink. He had come in before the show instead of after. When I got outside, he was sitting there drinking. I sang all his favorite songs to try to make up to him. The next time he said, "Ursa, baby," I let him do a little bit more of what he wanted, but this time he was the one who stopped himself.

"I'll wait till you ready," he had said, then he smiled a bit. "I started to say, I won't be ready till you are. But that would be a lie, Urs. I want you so much."

When he got up close to me, he was hot like a furnace. I backed away from him.

"If you won't have it this way, what about . . ."

I said no before he could finish.

"You didn't hear what I was going to say."

"I think I know."

"I'm going to ask you again."

I said nothing.

"All you act like you want from a man is a little peck on the cheek. Somebody ought to give you a little peck on the cheek, and I don't mean this one." He patted the side of my face.

I couldn't tell if he were angry or what. He pulled me back close to him.

I didn't let him inside me completely until the night we were married. I understood more than Mama knew about pushing a man out. He had never liked for me to sing that song "Open the Door, Richard" and I never would sing it after the first time because he'd said, "When are you going to let Richard in?" No, it wasn't so much he didn't like it as I felt uncomfortable singing it, or any song that had anything to do with opening up. I still sang the song about the tunnel closing tight around the train and the one about the bird woman who took this man on a long journey, but never returned him. "What's wrong, Ursa?" he'd keep asking, and even the night we were married, and he took me up to his room at the Drake Hotel, he'd kept asking, "What's wrong, baby? Ursa, honey, what's wrong?" He kept holding me and kissing me. We were both out of our clothes, but we'd done nothing yet.

"I can't, Mutt."

"Hell if you can't, you got a cunt, ain't you?"

I said nothing.

"What's wrong, baby? What do you call it?"

I still wouldn't answer.

The first time, a couple of months later, when I'd flared back at him with his own kind of words, he'd said, "You never used to talk like that. How'd you get to talk like that?"

I answered, "I guess you taught me. Corregidora taught Great Gram to talk the way she did."

"Don't give me hell, Ursa," he said now. "You know this is hell. Don't you feel anything? Don't you want me?"

"Yes," I said.

"I want to help you, but I can't help you unless you help me."

He had parted my legs, but I pushed him away.

"Any other man would say you was crazy. Any other man wouldn't put up with this shit."

"You don't have to." I hadn't meant to say it.

He'd started soothing me again, almost like one soothes a baby.

"I act like a child, don't I? Somebody told me even after I'd had a man, I'd still act like a child."

"You not a child. You something, but you not a child."

I let him get close to me again.

"Naw, Ursa, you ain't a child."

I let him get close till he was inside.

He kept asking me what he was doing to me, but I wouldn't tell him.

"What am I doing to you, Ursa . . . I'm fucking you, ain't I? What's wrong? Say it, Urs. I said I know you from way back. I'm fucking you, ain't I? Say it."

"Mutt, I . . ."

He laughed. "You ain't no hard woman, baby."

Stroking my hair, he came. "Are you still afraid of me?"

"Naw, Mutt."

"Are you sure, baby?"

"I'm sure."

He kissed my forehead.

May Alice had said that after you had a baby you felt like telling people. After I had had Mutt I felt like telling

people, but at the same time it was something that you
didn't tell, something that you kept inside. I think I was
happy then. I would sing songs that had to do with holding
things inside you. Secret happinesses, a tenderness. I think
Mutt was embarrassed by the way I would look at him.
Sometimes I would sing whole songs to him, and that's why
I would think he had gotten out of the habit of sitting as
close to the front as he did, but later I learned it was
because he wanted to watch the other men, how they were
reacting to me. I learned that it was because he'd got crazy
somehow on account of me. Once I'd said playfully, when
he brought the subject of the other men up, "You crazy,
man." He'd answered me equally as playful, "You crazy,
too, woman." But then it got so it wasn't playful anymore,
and he'd meant everything he said about those men.

"When Corregidora had that stroke he didn't call in his
men, he called in his women and said he'd give them any
amount of money they wonted if they take it off him, but
they said didn't none of them put it on him."

"Shit, I'm tired a hearing about Corregidora's women.
Why do you have to remember that old bastard anyway?"

I said nothing.

"You one of them," he said.

"What?"

"If you wasn't one of them you wouldn't like them mens
watching after you."

"They don't watch after me, Mutt."

"I wish you'd take that damned mascara off. It makes you
look like a bitch."

"The thunder sounds like it's talking, don't it?" I asked.

"That's because you got music all in your head. The
thunder ain't doing nothing but thundering."

"Naw, Mutt, it's talking. If you listen, you can hear it too."

"I seen the way Tyrone Davis was looking at you."

"He wasn't looking no way at me."

"A man don't like for other mens to look at they wives like that."

"Last night you didn't wont nobody to say nothing to me, and tonight they can't even look at me."

"Not the way mens look. A man know if a woman don't."

"Mutt, you crazy."

"You call me crazy again you gon see just how crazy I am."

I came home from work and he was laying across the bed in his shorts. He only went to my performances sometimes now, usually on Friday. We had been married about four months. It was near the end of March, and was just beginning to be warm in the day, but still cold at night. He hadn't turned the heat on, and didn't have a cover over him, and looked like he was freezing.

"Mutt, you'll catch your death."

I went over and lit the heater.

"What do you care? You got all them men."

"Mutt, you crazy."

He only looked at me this time. I hadn't meant to say it, and regretted it.

"Rub my thighs, baby."

"What's wrong with your thighs?"

"They tight. I been working all day. You know a man got to work. And working in tobacco ain't easy."

I felt he had some kind of trick, but I took my jacket off and went over to the bed and started massaging his thighs.

"Feel how tight they are."

"Yes." The muscles did feel tight.

C—K

"Get back behind there, you ain't rubbed behind there."

I rubbed behind his thighs.

"You ain't rubbed in between them."

I rubbed in between his thighs, and he kept telling me to move up just a little bit, and then he pulled me by the shoulders until I was up on top of him, and felt him through my skirt.

"You ain't had it this way, have you?"

"No."

He pushed me away real hard. "Well, you ain't getting it."

"Mutt."

That was when he first started to use that part of my feeling to try to pressure me into giving up the job. Whenever he wanted it and I didn't, he'd take me, because he knew that I wouldn't say, No, Mutt, or even if I had, sometimes I wonder about whether he would have taken me anyway. But those times that I wanted it, and he sensed that I wanted it, that's when he would turn away from me.

"Mutt."

"Take it someplace else."

"What if I do?"

He gave me a hard look. "Try me."

He made me think he was going to.

"My pussy, ain't it, Ursa?"

"Yes, Mutt, it's your pussy."

"My pussy, ain't it, baby?"

"Yes."

"Well, it's yours now."

He turned away.

Finally I got to the point where I tried to learn from him, play it his way. If he could be cold, I told myself, I could too. He'd been kind of funny about coming to the place lately. He'd come to the place, and kind of look around, like in those movies where those men come in and "case out a joint," one hand in his pocket, smoking a cigarette with the other hand, then he'd leave. But he never sat down at a table like he used to. He had moved from a front table while we were courting to a back table in the corner while he was watching who looked at me wrong, and then finally, just before he went and tried to grab me off the stage, he had begun to "case out the joint." If it had been anyone else, I mean, if I had been anyone else, and the consequences hadn't been like they were, seeing him standing there with his hand in his pocket, smoking that damned cigarette, would have made me laugh.

I was sitting on the edge of the bed. He had come in and cased out the joint, but then when I got home he wasn't even there. When he did come home he got undressed. I guess he must have thought I didn't want it, because he was going to give it to me. But this time I wasn't going to give it to him.

"What's the matter, Urs? Cat got your tongue? Cat or rat one. If the cat ain't got it, the rat have. What's the matter, woman!"

He was angry now, but he didn't try to force me in bed with him like I thought he would. And it was the first time I hadn't given it to him when *he* said yes. Maybe it was because I *did* want it.

"I'm just playing it your way," I said. "Something else I learned."

"My way or your own?" he asked.

No, he didn't force me down with him, and when I did want to give in he wouldn't take what I had to give.

"And that bastard you work for, he ain't no different from anybody else. He's all eyes too, and probably all dick."

It was after one of his joint casings. I said nothing.

"How many times you relieved his swelling? He ain't had you working there every night for nothing, have he?"

"Mutt, it ain't like that. He ain't tried nothing. He don't mean nothing to me."

"You got to mean something to him, though, way I see him looking."

"He ain't even really friendly. He's kind of shy, anyway."

"Them's the kind you got to watch out for. Play like he ain't friendly. But I bet he's got something friendly down there between his legs. Them's the kind womens come to anyway. The shy ones. I mean, since they don't come to the womens, the womens got to come to them."

"Like you?"

He said, "Shit."

The next night I heard some men laughing at Mutt. If he had ever heard it, he just didn't care. I was on my way up to the stage. It wasn't like a theater stage, but more like a reserved space in the floor, with a piano. I kind of stopped when I heard them. Mutt was standing near the back of the room, looking.

"What that nigger call hisself doing? Being Dick Tracy?"

The other man said softly, "That's his wife."

The man turned around. "Aw, scuse me."

I said nothing. I went on up to the stage.

Mutt must've spent several weeks acting that way. When I started singing, he would listen a little, look around again, and then leave. They have Shaft coats now. I guess he must've been wearing his Dick Tracy coat then. Yeah, if I was an outsider I probably would've laughed too. I just stood there trying not to let my embarrassment show in my voice. I sang "See See Rider." Somebody hollered, "Yeah, see what you have done, baby." "Tadpole gonna see see your behind out of here." "Let the woman sing," somebody else said. I sang "The Broken Soul Blues." People always got real quiet on that. Mutt left in the middle of "The Broken Soul Blues." Either he was getting disturbed in the mind, I was thinking, or he was just doing that to humiliate me. Naw, I didn't think he was crazy now, I just thought he was doing it all for spite.

When I came home he was turned over on his back. I asked him what was wrong. He said a man works hard all day and just gets tired sometime. I said nothing. Then he said something about a man working for a woman. He said, "A man works for a woman, a man don't work for hisself." I said, "A man's got to eat and have someplace to sleep too." He said, "A man sees to it that a woman eats and has some place to sleep, and *children*, if he got any, before he takes a bite or feels like he can lay his head down." I didn't say anything else to him. He asked me to come over and rub his back for him, to loosen up some of those tight muscles. I went over and rubbed his back. He fell asleep before I finished, or pretended he was asleep.

"That's what I'm gon do," he said. He was standing with his arms all up in the air. I was on my way to work. "One a y'all wont to bid for her? Piece a ass for sale. I got me a piece a ass for sale. That's what y'all wont, ain't it? Piece a ass. I said I got a piece a ass for sale, anybody wont to bid on it?"

"Mutt, you wouldn't."

"You think I won't. I'ma be down there tonight, and as soon as you get up on that stage, I'ma sell me a piece a ass."

I walked out the door.

Mutt was there. I'd started to tell Tadpole what he planned to do, but I didn't. I was afraid if I did, Mutt might not go through with it, and then there I'd be, looking like a fool anyway. I thought the best thing to do would be just to sing loud, and have Tadpole put him out when and if he started something. I was glad so far he hadn't started a fight with a man. I'd been expecting that, but instead he'd come in looking like damn Dick Tracy, making men rather laugh at him than fight him anyway.

Mutt wasn't there when the show started, but he came in the middle. I was singing one of Ella Fitzgerald's songs, and as soon as I saw him I kind of gradually increased the volume, hoping people wouldn't notice. The piano player, though, must've thought I was crazy, but he played a little louder too. A few men, I think, who had started waiting for Mutt to come in, looked around and saw him and kind of smiled. I was scared too, but I was still singing, and calling his bluff. I saw him raise his arm, and just keep it suspended in the air. Instead of saying anything, he just let it drop, and put his hand in his pocket and left. I ended the song loud anyway. And then I sang a very soft one.

When I got home he was sitting at the dresser. He didn't turn around to look at me because he could see me through the mirror. I closed the door and stood looking at him.

"I'm glad you didn't, Mutt."

"It wasn't on account of you, it was on account of my great-grandaddy. Seeing as how he went through all that for his woman, he wouldn't have appreciated me selling you off."

"Well, for whatever reason, I'm glad. I was hoping it was for me, though." I went to hang up my jacket.

"Don't act Missy," he said, angry.

"What are you talking about?"

"Don't act Miss Missy with me. I ain't *your* slave neither."

"I didn't say you was. I haven't treated you like you was."

He'd turned from the dresser and got up. He was standing looking at me real wild, like he would do something.

"I didn't say you was," I repeated.

I was looking hurt now, at least I felt hurt. And I was also afraid of him.

"I ain't looking for no argument," he said, and walked out, slamming the door.

I must've been asleep when he came back. I could only feel him getting up in the morning, getting ready to go to work. He had to be there at eight.

"They got a big-time band from Chicago coming out to Dixieland," Mutt said. "You think ole Crawdad'll let you off Friday night?"

He was acting more like himself, but lately I'd gotten into the habit of being cautious.

"His name ain't Crawdad, it's Tadpole."

"Crawdad or Tadpole, they both swim around in the same hole," he said, but not sarcastic. He was still in good spirits.

"I think I can get off," I said coolly.

"Come on, Ursa, baby, don't act that way. We need a little night out together, don't you think?"

I nodded.

"Come on over here, honey. Don't stand up there looking like that."

I went over to the bed, and sat down beside him. We made love and then slept. He was asleep before I was.

The big band from Chicago was probably the best group they'd had out there, but then I'd never really gone much, so I couldn't be a judge. Most of the time when they had something out there I was working myself. And then again my joy might have been just being with Mutt, acting the good way he was, and that got into the band's music. I couldn't jitterbug well and so Mutt and me mostly slow-danced. Mutt called it "two-stepping."

"You can't jitterbug?" Mutt asked.

"No, I never really got a chance to learn it."

"Well, you move good and easy this way though."

I didn't like what he was doing now. He was getting up really close to me, more like you see people doing in back alleys than on the dance floor, even though there were other people dancing pretty close. But what he was doing made me think of what people did in the bedroom. He kept making me feel him hard against me, and trying to fit himself in my crotch, and I kept moving a little to the side.

"Be still, woman."

"Mutt, please."

He was holding my shoulders tight, so that even if I hadn't been too embarrassed to move away from him, I couldn't have. Each time he would try to fit himself between my legs, I would move a little to the side. I know we must have looked bad to some people and funny to others.

"Mutt, we ain't in bed."

"You act the same way when we are."

He talked a little louder than I did.

"Mutt, I'm so embarrassed I don't know what to do."

When the song ended I was so embarrassed I wouldn't even look at people. We went over and sat down. I kept looking down at my beer glass. He was drinking rum cola.

"Mutt, I just don't understand you," I said, looking up at him.

"You mumbling, Ursa."

"I said I don't understand," I said a little louder, almost speaking through my teeth.

"You don't try," he said, and took a drink.

When the next slow song came on he wanted to dance again, but I wouldn't. He got up anyway and held out his hand to me, but I wouldn't take it. He kept looking at me real hard, like he was saying, "Take it, bitch. You better take my hand." He wasn't saying it, but it was all in his eyes. And after that was in his eyes, "Don't embarrass me, woman," was in his eyes, and then the hard hateful look was there again. I'd taken his hand when the "Don't embarrass me this way, woman" look had come into his eyes, and we were up on the dance floor when the hard hateful look was back again.

"Don't do that to me no more, Urs," he said.

I shook my head, and let him hold my shoulder hard, and try to grind himself into me. I swore, though, that if he asked me to dance again, I'd run in the bathroom before I'd get up on the floor with him. When the song ended, I could feel his hand move down to my behind. I saw some man look at me and smile. I didn't look at him again.

"How you doing, buddy?" somebody asked Mutt.

"I'm doing, man. How you doing?"

"I'm doing, too," the man answered.

I sat down, not looking at people. Then it was the part of the show where they asked somebody from the audience who could sing to come up to the stage. I'd forgotten about that part of the show. I'd never gone up the few times I was there, but I'd still forgotten. Tonight they asked if there was a female vocalist in the house.

"Go on up, Urs, don't be shy," Mutt said, pushing me a little on the shoulder.

I saw some people looking my way.

"No, Mutt," I said quiet, trying to give him the "Don't embarrass me this way, man" look, but it didn't come off.

"Go on up, Urs, you can sing."

I got up from the table and went in the ladies' room. I saw people's eyes following me like they thought I was going up to the stage at first, and when they discovered I wasn't they just kept watching me. When I came out of the ladies' room, that part of the show was over, and Mutt was standing outside with his arms folded, looking evil.

"Take you a age to pee?" he asked.

"No."

"Get your coat, we going home."

I got my coat, and we left. When we got home he slammed the door.

"You ain't got no right to be mad at me," I said.

He had that hard hateful look again.

"If you ever see me hold my hand out to you in a public place you better take it," he said. "I don't care what you do here, but if we ever in a public place, you better take my hand."

"You didn't have no right to act like you was in the bedroom."

"I wasn't dancing no different from the way other peoples was dancing."

"I didn't see no other people dancing like that. Close, but not like that."

"It look different than it feel, baby."

"You didn't have no right to put your hand on me, though, not where people could see."

"I didn't even touch nothing but your shoulders. Shit."

"Yes, you did. When that song was over you had your hand on my behind, right where people could see."

"Well, it's my ass, ain't it? When I screwed you last night and asked you whose ass it was, you said it was mine. Ain't no other man had it, or have they?"

"Mutt, that was different. You know it." I felt like I was going to cry, but I wouldn't, not in front of him.

"What made it different?"

"Cause people saw it. Cause we wasn't in here, that's why."

"Shit, you my wife, ain't you? We married, ain't we?"

I said nothing. He kept looking at me, almost like he was half grinning, half making fun of me. I turned away a little. I thought I was going to cry, but I didn't. I turned back. "You wont to show everybody when we out in public that you got your . . . piece—but when we here you act like you ain't got shit. I ain't no more than a piece a shit. Well, you got your piece a shit. I can play your game too, buddy. Tomorrow night you can just come on down to the place and sell your piece a shit, cause I don't give a damn."

I turned and went out the door. I went down to the hotel lobby and waited till I was in the toilet, and then I cried.

When I came back he was in bed. He didn't turn toward me, and I didn't tell him good night. He waited until I'd turned the light off before he hit back at me. "I was just pretend fucking, baby, like you used to do. Wasn't doing nothing but play fucking."

When he came to the place the next night, it wasn't to sell his piece a shit, it was to try to take it off the stage, and then when his piece a shit wouldn't get off the stage and Tadpole and some other men put him out, it was to knock that piece a shit down some stairs. I should have known something was wrong when he came home from work that night. He'd brought a bottle of bourbon with him. I was on my way out. It was a Saturday night in April.

"When you get there, Urs, just go over to one a they tables for me, and kinda lean down, you know how you can kinda lean down so you show a little bit of them titties, and then just ask one of em what he wont. If you don't know what he's gonna say, I do. 'Piece a ass, please.' 'Piece a whose ass?' 'Yours, good-lookin woman.' "

"Mutt, it ain't like that."

"Tell me if they ain't asked?"

He was all up in my face now, squeezing that bottle in that brown paper sack. I told him I'd be damned if I'd tell him a damn thing.

Mutt came in with his hands in his pockets, drunk this time. The other nights he had been a sober Dick Tracy, but tonight he looked like he couldn't hardly stand. When he started walking toward me I didn't think he would keep coming, but he did. He was within a few feet of me when I stopped singing, the look in his eyes somewhere between the mean and hateful and "Don't embarrass me this way" look. He didn't have his hand out, though. He had them both in his pockets.

"Come on, you going home," he said.

I didn't move.

"I said you going home."

I still didn't move. The place had got real quiet.

"What's wrong with that man?" somebody asked.

"He's crazy," somebody else answered.

"Already crazy, he don't need to be drunk, too," another said.

Mutt turned quickly and looked in the direction where the voices came from, and then turned back to me.

"Woman, you heard me."

I said nothing.

"You my woman, ain't you?"

I kept looking at him. I couldn't make out his look, and I was too embarrassed right now to look anywhere else. He still didn't hold his hand out, though. He seemed like he'd planted them more firmly in his pockets.

"You ain't they woman, is you?"

I stood looking at him. He almost had the "Don't embarrass me this way" look, but the mean and hateful one kept getting in the way. The hard look won.

"Bitch, you coming home," he said and grabbed for me. He almost stumbled and some men grabbed him. While they was taking him out he was saying, "You ain't they woman, is you? Is you they woman, or mines?" The men got him out the door. Tadpole came over to me and asked if I was okay, if I wanted to stop, but I said naw, I was all right. I finished out the show. Mutt kept peeking in, the mean and hateful look on his face, his collar pulled up. And then it was when I was on my way home, he knocked his piece a shit down those stairs.

"You was cussing everybody out," Tadpole said. "They said they didn't know *what* you was."

He was standing up over me in the hospital, the first person I didn't think was Mutt.

I don't remember what I said in the hospital, but Tadpole told me later that I kept saying something about a man treat a woman like a piece a shit.

"You got your piece a shit now, ain't you? You got your piece a shit now."

IV

It was June 1969. I was forty-seven, still working at the Spider. I walked by one of the tables on my way to the stage.

"I wont you to put me in the alley tonight, sister," one of the men said. He was drunk.

"Will do."

"Next best thang to the blues is a good screw."

I sat down at the piano.

"Show business is funny, ain't it?"

I started singing a song, hoping that would make him quiet. It did. I put him where he wanted to get. I sang a low down blues. It surprised me he stayed quiet throughout the whole show, otherwise Logan would have throwed him out. When I finished, though, he came up to me. "Can I bring you over to my table? Come on over to my table and have a drink with me." I went over with him. I'd handled drunks before, and he didn't seem like a dangerous drunk. I sat down and he asked me what I drank. I said beer. He ordered me a beer.

"Show business is funny, ain't it?" he repeated.

I said, "Yeah, it's funny."

"I'm sanging over at the Drake Hotel," he said. "I'm fifty-eight years old and just got my first job sanging over at the

Drake Hotel, and I been sanging all my life. Show business is sho funny, ain't it?"

I nodded and drank.

"Before then I had to go around with a paper sack. They let you sang in their places, but I have to go around with a paper sack. Some people don't understand that. They say you looking for a handout. But I ain't looking for a handout. I been sanging all my life, and just got my first job yesterday sanging over at the Drake Hotel."

I said nothing.

"You come over there and see me, won't you?"

I nodded, but I knew I wouldn't.

"You won't forget where it's at, will you?"

"I know where it's at."

"Yeah, I been sanging all my life. You know how long Thelonius Monk was playing in that place all that long time before they discovered him. You know, I don't like to use that word 'discovered,' cause it's already there, ain't it?"

I nodded.

"Yes, indeedy, it's already there, but don't seem like they can see it. I don't know how many years daddy Monk was playing funk before they seen him. I call him daddy Monk because I wrote a song about it. I like to write my own songs, you know. I sing some of the others too, but I like to write my own. And I'm fifty-eight years old. You know, I don't like that word 'discovery.' Ray Charles is a genius, you know that? But let me tell you something and I don't have to spell it out for you cause you know what I'm talking about. Sinatra was the first one to call Ray Charles a genius, he spoke of 'the genius of Ray Charles.' And after that everybody called him a genius. They didn't call him a genius before that though. He *was* a genius but they didn't call him that. You know what I'm trying to tell you?

If a white man hadn't told them, they wouldn't've seen it. If I come and told them they wouldn't've seen it. Do you know what I'm talking about? I could've told 'em. You could've told 'em. Like, you know, they say Columbo discovered America, he didn't discover America. You hear that song where Aretha say she discovered Ray Charles. Now tha's awright." He laughed.

I laughed too.

"I could tell them about you, but they wouldn't listen. And you could come over there and tell them about me, but they wouldn't listen." He stopped, then he said, "You know you made me feel good sanging. You made me feel real good sanging."

He didn't give me time to say thank you. He went on: "You know the onliest other time I felt good was when I was in the Apollo Theater. That was a long time ago cause I ain't been back to New York in a long time. But the Lady was singing. Billie Holiday. She sang for two solid hours. And then when she finished, there was a full minute of silence, just silence. And then there was applauding and crying. She came out and was nervous for a full thirty-two seconds. And then she sang. And you see what they done to her, don't you?"

I said, "Yes."

"If you listen to those early records and then listen to that last one, you see what they done to her voice. They say she destroyed herself, but she didn't destroy herself. They destroyed her."

He was almost across the table at me, then he stopped, and sat back, as if he were exhausted. All the time he was talking, I could see Logan eyeing us, as if he were ready to come over any moment at my signal.

"It's a sin, ain't it? It's a sin and a shame. Naw it ain't a shame. It's shameful. That's what it is, it's shameful."

I didn't really see the difference then, but I nodded. He took another drink. He was drinking T-bird. Then he sat looking at me.

"I bet you got some good pussy."

I said nothing. I really hadn't expected that. I just looked back at him.

"Tell me if you ain't got some good pussy."

I didn't tell him anything. I just kept looking at him.

"I don't mean to get nasty," he said. "I just think you a good-looking woman." He leaned toward me. "Tell me if you ain't got some good pussy."

I wanted to go, but I just sat there, saying nothing. He sat back again.

"I know you got some good pussy," he said, as if he were giving a verdict.

A man we called Cat's-eye Marble because he had a popped eye, passed by the table. I said hi to him. He said, "You looking prosperous, baby, real prosperous." That was his favorite word. He went on by. I looked back at the man. He was frowning, still looking at me.

"You won't forget the name of it, will you?" he asked.

I said I wouldn't forget it.

"You be over to hear me, won't you?" he asked.

I nodded.

"I ain't going to be there but for two weeks. They only signed me on for two weeks."

I said nothing. He was silent. He drank some more wine.

"Did I make you mad?" he asked.

I said, Naw, he didn't make me mad.

"I didn't mean to get nasty with you. I ain't got nasty with a woman a day in my life, and I didn't mean to get nasty with you." He got up rocking. I started to ask him if he was all right, but didn't. "You stay sweet, you hear?"

I said I would. I told him to take it easy.

"You won't forget, will you?" he asked.

I said No I wouldn't forget. Then I nodded to Logan, who came and helped him outside. I went back to the piano.

"... *She liked me to fan her thighs when it was hot and then one day she had me fan her between her legs. Then after that she made me sleep with her, cause, you know, he wouldn't sleep with her, and then after that something went wrong with her. She had some hot prongs she come after me with, and she told me to raise up my dress and I know where she was going to put them, right between my legs. Cause she knew he was getting his from me too. But then that was when he came in. He grabbed her and knocked the prongs out of her hands and then he started beating her. That woman was black for days to come. After that he just kept her locked up in that bedroom and wouldn't even let me go near her. I guess she thought of it that way, the prongs I mean, from having me fan her between her legs. Thought of it that way in her mind. She just went crazy, that's all. Short time after that, she died up there. But there was a lots of thangs like that that was going on where the husband just let his wife do what she did, or he do it hisself if he was ready for some new pussy. But then lots of time too he just wont the one pussy and do like Corregidora did.*

"... *He fucked her and fucked me. He would've fucked you and your mama if y'all been there and he wasn't old and crooked up like he got. Mama ran off cause he would've killed her. I don't know what she did. She never would tell me what she did. Up till today she still won't tell me what it was she did. He would've killed her, though, if she hadn't gone. He raised me and then when I got big enough he started fucking me. Seem like he raised me fucking me.*

Yeah, Mama told me how in the old days he was just buying up women. They'd have to raise up their dress so he could see what they had down there, and he feel all around down there, and then he feel their bellies to see if they had solid bellies. And they had to be pretty. He wasn't buying up them fancy mulatta womens though. They had to be black and pretty. They had to be the color of his coffee beans. That's why he said he always liked my mama better than me. But he never said nothing about what it was she did to him. What is it a woman can do to a man that make him hate her so bad he wont to kill her one minute and keep thinking about her and can't get her out of his mind the next?"

I hadn't seen Sal Cooper much since I walked out. We'd see each other on the street sometimes downtown. We were polite, but we never stopped and talked. I usually kept to my end of town, going to work, then back to the apartment, except when I had groceries to get or some shopping to do downtown. But I rarely did shopping downtown. The drugstore on the corner had most of the things I needed and the grocery store down the road. I made most of the gowns I sang in and I wasn't one for changing costumes a lot. So that I'd only run into Tadpole maybe three or four times. We didn't speak or even acknowledge each other. I heard from somebody that he and Vivian got together, and then about five years ago he sold the place and moved to Chicago. Yeah, and the papers came for me to sign. I was a free woman again, whatever that meant. Sal Cooper I'd heard stayed on at the place when the new owner came. His name was Austin Bradley and he was from Columbus, Ohio. I heard that he was going to change the name of the place, but as far as I knew, it still had the same name. And people were still talking about going over to Happy's. He was going to call it some kind of club but I reckon he figured it was successful enough with its old name, so he just kept it. I think he imported some woman from Detroit to come in and do the singing. Some woman from one of them big cities up North. I think maybe it was Detroit or maybe it's just I keep Detroit on my mind, cause that's the only place I been out of Kentucky. Anyway, what's funny is when he first got there, he come over here and heard me sing and offered me a job singing over there. I told him, Naw thank you anyway but I had my job. I didn't tell him nothing else, but he musta found out about it when he went back over there and started talking to Sal. And then shortly after that he imported that woman from someplace up North. But I bet Sal must've been surprised when he said who it was he asked. Well, I was surprised myself him asking me, though some people say I don't look my age, I look younger than my age. I just tell them it's hereditary. I be forty-eight in June. Well, I never saw Cat no more. I didn't even hear anything about her till I saw Jeffrene that time. Yeah, Jeffrene's grown up now. They calling her Miss Jeffrene, except her mama, her mama still call her Jeffy or sometimes Jeff. I'd see her on the street, and she wouldn't speak and I wouldn't speak. Except one time I seen her she stop, like she was going to say something, but I started on by. She was standing out in front of the Freeze and Eli's dime store over on Third Street. I'd been down to the appliance store over there to pay a bill, and come out and there she was. She kind of jumped when she seen me, and stopped, but I was still going.

"Just walk on by," she said. "That's right. Just walk on by."

I started to, but then I didn't. I stopped to see what she had to say. I figured if I didn't like it, I could just go on.

I stood there looking at her. I must have been looking hostile because she said, "I ain't lookin for no argument."

"What is it?" I asked, still standing there. I think I had my hands on my hips or folded or something.

"I was sick with pneumonia. Didn't nobody come to see me but Mama. I got thinner. Did you notice?"

She did look thinner, but I didn't say I noticed. She had on blue jeans like she always wore, except when you seen her coming from work. She worked out at the narcotics hospital out there on Versailles Road. She was a nurses' aide, I think somebody told me. Now she had on blue jeans. They looked like they were a little too big for her.

I said nothing.

"Cat got your tongue?" She grinned. "She always used to wish she had it."

I looked away from her at the traffic light. She was standing close to the building and I was standing out on the sidewalk. Someone passed by and pushed me a little closer toward her. Then I stood next to the building, but away from her.

"You scared of me, ain't you?"

"Naw, I'm not afraid of you."

She said nothing, then she looked at me and smiled. "I don't think I'm taking too much for granted if I say you are."

"Jeffy, I've got to go."

"I seen Cat."

"How is she?"

"You care?"

I said nothing.

"I seen her down in Versailles."

"I thought she went to Midway."

"Well, when I seen her she was in Versailles. She don't

look too good. She start looking her age now, or letting herself look her age. I told her she better get her shit together. She was in a accident, you know."

I grimaced. "What kind of a accident?"

"She work over at the Wax Works, you know. One that makes Dixie Cups or something like that. She was reaching down to get something and got her hair caught in one of these machines and it pulled all her hair out. Well, it pulled all the top part out. Might as well say all of it. She was in the hospital about six months. What you looking like that for? You didn't care nothing about her."

"I do care."

"You could've fooled me."

"I don't mean that the way you want to take it."

"I don't want to take it any way. I wouldn't mind you giving me some."

My eyes hardened.

"Well, I'ma tell you about Cat," she continued. "She wearing that wig. She sued the company, and now they got to buy all her wigs for her. Shit, I told her I'd go down there and pick me one of them good wigs. I wouldn't be wearing one of them shitty wigs like she got. You can tell she got a wig on. I'd go down there and pick me out one of them wigs you couldn't tell was a wig."

"Is she all right?"

"Scalp healed all up. She said you can still see where it all come out though. I ast her to show it to me, but she wouldn't show it to me. I said I thought we meant more to each other than that, but she still wouldn't let me see it. I couldn't even touch her head. Now, you know that ain't right."

I said nothing. She kept looking at me.

"Bad thing to happen to a woman, ain't it?"

I looked at her, trying to keep my eyes hard.

"Things like that," she said. "That kind of thing makes you don't feel like a woman."

"When are you going to stop lying?" I asked. I had turned away from her and was looking in the store window.

"I didn't know I'd started," she said.

I said nothing.

"You didn't come to see me when I had pneumonia."

"I didn't even know you had pneumonia." I hadn't meant to say it. I don't know why I did. I stood very close to the window so she wouldn't see my eyes.

"I hope that woman gets her ass together," she said. "I kept telling her to get her ass together. Ain't no use a her bleeding over that shit, I said. I told her to get her ass together and keep it together."

"What did she say?"

"I think she was glad I told her."

She turned, looking with me into the window. She didn't get close to me as I thought she would, because I had kind of jumped. If she'd noticed it, she didn't let on. We were both silent for a long time.

"I used to come in here and buy those little dime banks they got in there," she said. "You know those little dime banks they sell?"

"Yeah."

"They got penny ones too. I didn't like the penny ones so much as the dime ones. They got some that you have to wait till you get ten dollars in them before they open up. Then they got some got a hole in the bottom, you can get your money out anytime. I used to like the ones you had to wait for."

I said nothing.

"I knew there wasn't nothing between y'all," she said. "I knew it even if you didn't."

I played like I didn't know who she meant. And then, I was thinking, maybe I didn't.

"I don't have to listen to you," I said quietly.

"Who do you listen to?"

I said nothing.

"Do you have anybody?"

I wouldn't answer.

"You know I got something for you when you ready for it."

"I don't want no shit from you, Jeffy."

"Woman like you got to get something, ain't she?"

I turned and walked away from her. She said it softly, but I still heard. "You *know* it felt good that time."

I looked back at her quickly, but walked on.

"Gonna be hard for you, baby," she said. "Ursa?"

"What?" I stopped, but didn't turn around.

"Maybe you can go see her? Maybe you can help her get her ass together."

She said it like she meant it, but still it strangled any impulse I'd had to go see Catherine. And after that day, whenever I saw Jeffrene, I'd cross the street.

I'd never seen Jeffrene with anybody myself, but somebody said she was going with one of the women patients down at the narcotics hospital. A couple of years back she had been being seen with a man from Versailles, but things hadn't worked out.

V

"You just showed that man your ass, didn't you? You could've tried to understand, tried to help him. But all you did was show him your ass. He wanted to help you."

I said nothing. Jim was standing up by the piano waving his hands at me.

"You show your ass to these mens and then when they try to get on it, you say Uh-uh, uh-uh." He kept waving his hands.

Logan came over and wanted to put him out. But I said No. When he went and talked to Max, Max came and said he wanted to put him out for good. But I said maybe they should just put him out for now.

"You don't care nothing, don't wont to know nothing," Jim said. Logan had him by the arm. "Just had your ass all up in his face."

Max waved for me to start playing so it would drown out what Jim was saying.

After that, whenever Jim came in, I wouldn't say nothing to him and he wouldn't say nothing to me. He stopped drinking so much where he got drunk. I guess he must've remembered what it was he said, but he didn't apologize. He just come in and drink just enough and then leave. Logan keep eyeing him though, and every now and then

Max'll come and ask me if Jim keeping his head. I just say
Yeah. Seem like every time I look up, though, there's Jim.
Least once a week. He be looking at me, but he don't
bother me. He don't bother me and I don't bother him.
Sometimes he be looking at me, though, like he's studying
me or something, but then I give him a hard look and he
look away. I don't ask him who he's studying, I just give
him that hard look. I guess I could say something to him,
but then I got in the habit of not, and just kept it. I guess
he got in the habit of not too—just studying me every now
and then.

I won't say I don't think of Mutt Thomas, because I do.
But I ain't seen him in twenty-two years, and don't know if
I know him if I did. I don't know if I know Jim if I didn't
see him every time I turn around. But sometimes I find
myself wonting to look at Jim to see if they's any Mutt in
him, but I don't. Well, what this is all building up to, anyway, is that Sal Cooper came in the other day. I just about
peed on myself when I looked up and saw her, but I know
it was me she wanted. Wouldn't be no other reason she be
in here. I finished out the song I was singing and came over
there where she was. Now Monroe let me play however
way I wanted to, except the regular straight two hours
Friday and Saturday show. I couldn't just stop in the middle of them. But I just stopped and came over where Sal
was and sat down.

"I seen Mutt th'other day," she said.

"Why you telling me?"

"Cause I know how you still feel about him."

"Do you?"

"I knew how you feeled about him when you married
Tadpole. I don't think Tadpole knew how you feeled at
first, and I don't think you knew how you feeled."

"I knew exactly how I felt. I hated him."

She smiled but said nothing. Then she said, "At least you used the past tense."

"It's been a long time. I don't know how I'd feel. I don't know what I'd do. I still resent him."

"I know you ain't took no other man on."

"What right have you to . . ." I stopped. If it had been Cat I never would have started.

"I'm telling you because I seen him. He was over to the place. He can come in now, you know."

"I can imagine."

"I didn't even recognize him at first. He had this beard and look like a old man, look older than he is. I didn't know him till he come over and said 'Sal.' I said, 'That you, Mutt Thomas?' He said, 'Yeah.' Then I looked behind all that hair and seen it was Mutt. I told him you wasn't there. He said he know you wasn't. I didn't tell him where you was. But I figure he know, and be over here. I just wanted to tell you that he was coming."

"Thank you."

"You mad at me?"

"Naw I'm not mad."

"You something at me."

"I just said thank you, that's all. What do you want me to say?"

"You something at *him* then."

"I don't know what I am at him. I won't know till I see him. If he come."

"You don't think he's coming?"

"Yeah, I b'lieve he's coming. I don't know why I said that."

Sal stood up.

"Thank you," I said.

She didn't say anything, she just looked at me, then she went out.

Jim didn't come in that evening. If he had I would have talked to him. I don't know what I was feeling. A numbness. I knew I wanted to see Mutt, but I didn't know what it would be. I was excited, yes, that's what I was. I was excited about it. Mutt didn't come that evening nor the next evening. Jim didn't come either. It was a week before Mutt came. I knew him even with the beard. He wasn't heavier. He seemed solider. But I would have known him even if Sal hadn't prepared me. It was the Saturday-night show, so I couldn't stop. I sang on. I knew I was singing to him. I think he knew it too. But I knew I hadn't forgiven him. Even when I felt excited about seeing him, I knew I hadn't forgiven him too. I think he knew that as well, even when I finished and came over to the table. He said nothing. I said, "How are you, Mutt?" He nodded, and ordered me a beer, but he still didn't speak. When he did speak finally, he said, "Jim been writing me and telling me every now and nen how you getting along." I remembered that time when I thought Jim had been spying on me. But I wouldn't have used that word now. I just wondered who else Jim might have kept up on how things were going with me, because when I did feel I had to tell Mama my song, she listened, but it was the quiet kind of listening one has when they already know, or maybe just when it's a song they've sung themselves, but with different lyrics. As far as as I knew about her and Mr. Floyd, though, he was keeping to his side of the road, and she kept to hers. She said he was constantly asking her to make him some strawberry preserves, but that was all she'd done. And she never told me about any other man. She had written me something about having left a certain world behind her. I wasn't sure what she meant, but was sure that only one man could remake that world. My father.

"What does he tell you?" I asked.

"That you've still got your voice, that you're still Ursa."

I didn't tell him I'd known he was coming.

I drank my beer. I looked at the table, then at him.

"I want you to come back," he said.

I wanted to say I can't come back, but I couldn't say anything. I just looked at him. I didn't know yet what I would do. I knew what I still felt. I knew that I still hated him. Not as bad as then, not with that first feeling, but an after feeling, an aftertaste, or like an odor still in a room when you come back to it, and it's your own. I don't know what he saw in my eyes. His were different now. I can't explain how. I felt that now he wouldn't demand the same things. He'd demand different kinds of things. But there'd still be demands.

"Did you hear me?"

"I heard."

"What do you say?"

I didn't take my eyes from him. "Yes."

"I'm staying over at the old place," he said. I knew he meant the Drake. "I've got a job over at the Greenwood Cemetery. I know it's not the kind of job that . . . I was working in tobacco up in Connecticut. They got tobacco farms up there. Did you know that?"

I said I didn't know.

"Yeah. But then I just got tired of tobacco, I got tired of the smell, and I came back here. That's the first job I could get till I get something else. You know what I mean?"

I nodded.

"You remember my great-grandfather I told you about?" he asked. "The one with the wife?"

"Yeah."

"After they took her, when he went crazy he wouldn't eat nothing but onions and peppermint. Eat the onions so people wouldn't come around him, and then eat the peppermint so they would. I tried it but it didn't do nothing but make me sick."

I said nothing.

"You ready?" he asked.

I said I was. I told Max good night and went back with Mutt.

It wasn't the same room, but the same place. The same feel of the place. I knew what he wanted. I wanted it too. We didn't speak. We got out of our clothes. I got between his knees.

"You never would suck it," he was saying. "You never would suck it when I wanted you to. Oh, baby, you never would suck it. I didn't think you would do this for me."

It had to be sexual, I was thinking, it had to be something sexual that Great Gram did to Corregidora. I knew it had to be sexual: "What is it a woman can do to a man that make him hate her so bad he wont to kill her one minute and keep thinking about her and can't get her out of his mind the next?" In a split second I knew what it was, in a split second of hate and love I knew what it was, and I think he might have known too. A moment of pleasure and excruciating pain at the same time, a moment of broken skin but not sexlessness, a moment just before sexlessness, a moment that stops just before sexlessness, a moment that stops before it breaks the skin: "I could kill you."

I held his ankles. It was like I didn't know how much was me and Mutt and how much was Great Gram and Corregidora—like Mama when she had started talking like Great Gram. But was what Corregidora had done to *her*, to *them*, any worse than what Mutt had done to me, than what we had done to each other, than what Mama had done to Daddy, or what he had done to her in return, making her walk down the street looking like a whore?

"I could kill you."

He came and I swallowed. He leaned back, pulling me up by the shoulders.

"I don't want a kind of woman that hurt you," he said.

"Then you don't want me."

"I don't want a kind of woman that hurt you."

"Then you don't want me."

"I don't want a kind of woman that hurt you."

"Then you don't want me."

He shook me till I fell against him crying. "I don't want a kind of man that'll hurt me neither," I said.

He held me tight.

Praise for *The Healing*

Shortlisted for the 1998 National Book Award

"Gripping, beautiful, and well worth the wait" *Ms.* magazine

"Cause for hope, sustenance and even celebration" *New York Times*

"A major literary event . . . surprising, romantic and wholly satisfying" *Newsweek*

"With this wily, witty testimony of good and bad faith, Jones triumphantly reenters the fray – a trickster, a writer, and, with great fortune, a healer" *Boston Globe*

"Like Chaucer long before her, Jones continues the transformation of the face of fiction with the truth of the spoken word" *San Jose Mercury News*

Gayl Jones's first novel, *Corregidora*, now reprinted, won her recognition as a writer whose work was gripping, subtle, and sure. The publication of *The Healing*, her first novel in over twenty years, is a literary event.

Harlan Jane Eagleton is a faith healer, traveling by bus to small towns, converting sceptics, restoring minds and bodies. But before that she was a rock star's manager and before that a beautician. Harlan draws us constantly deeper into her world and the mystery at the heart of her tale – the story of her first healing.

The Healing is a lyrical exploration of the struggle to let go of pain, anger and love. Gayl Jones's ability to capture the sounds and moods of the American South makes her one of the crucial American writers of our times.